WILD HEX

TYSON WILD BOOK FIFTY NINE

TRIPP ELLIS

1

"**H**ey, Jackass! That's my space."

The gorgeous blonde was clearly upset.

It was an honest mistake.

We'd pulled into the parking lot at *Waffle Wizard*. Jack had zipped the Porsche into a space just as a big black F-150 pulled out. Waiting on the other side of the truck was a hot-hatch GR Corolla in Heavy Metal Gray with its yellow blinker flashing. I could see why the young lady was pissed off. She shouted through the passenger side window of her car as she pulled parallel with Jack's Ruby Star 911 GTS convertible.

Jack looked around, unimpressed. "I don't see your name on it."

The blonde scowled at him. "I had my blinker on."

The lot was packed, and cars circled like vultures for a space. It was a popular spot for breakfast. Waffle Wizard had every imaginable type of waffles, pancakes, muffins, you name it. Blueberry, strawberry, raspberry, even peanut butter. Drenched in butter and maple syrup, it was a caloric overload. I think it was better than *Waffle World.* Saturday morning drew the hung overcrowd, of which we were among.

"I didn't see you," Jack replied.

The blonde huffed and drove away, shouting one last remark that filtered through the open window. "Prick!"

JD's face scrunched up. "I think she was talking to you."

I gave him a doubtful glance. "You could have given her the space."

"I would have considered it if she'd have asked nicely."

I added, "She was cute."

"Yeah, well, I'm hungry."

We stepped across the parking lot and pushed into the restaurant. The delightful aroma of breakfast swirled. Forks clinked against plates, and conversation filled the room. The cheery hostess greeted us and put JD's name on the list. I flashed my badge, but it didn't make a table open up any quicker.

The angry blonde stepped in a few moments after us. She pretended not to notice and kept averting her eyes. She was really cute. Dare I say hot.

She had an angelic face with wispy blonde hair, fair skin, full lips, and eyes as deep as the Atlantic. She was an all-natural beauty. She didn't wear much, if any, makeup. There were no lip fillers or Botox injections. At her age, she didn't need them. One look, and you'd find yourself short of breath and suffering heart palpitations. A few other thoughts might enter your mind as well. Ones that might not be so angelic.

I was about to apologize when...

"Donovan, party of two," the hostess shouted.

She escorted us to a booth by the window, and we slid into the bench seats across from each other.

I sat facing the door, and I couldn't help but watch the stunning blonde as she waited to be seated.

"Enjoy your meal, gentlemen," the hostess said as she dealt out the menus, then darted back to the stand.

JD and I perused the menu, deciding on breakfast. Blueberry waffles, drenched in maple syrup with hash browns and bacon, sounded like a good idea to me. It was the kind of place where it was easy to order more than you could ever eat. My stomach rumbled, and I had a healthy appetite.

I watched with disappointment as the hostess sat the blonde across the restaurant from us. No chance for another casual encounter. No chance to apologize for the situation. A missed opportunity.

The waitress swung by our table and filled our cups with steaming coffee. The aroma of hot java swirled.

I decided to take the opportunity to get up, march across the restaurant, and introduce myself. I mean, how much worse could it go? We already started off on the wrong foot. I had nothing to lose.

I excused myself from the table.

JD looked at me with confusion.

Just as I stood up, my phone buzzed my pocket. I shouldn't have answered, but I did. It was a call from Sheriff Daniels. His gruff voice barked into the phone. "Where are you two nitwits?"

"We're on vacation," I said, trying to shirk my responsibilities.

"No, you're not. I didn't authorize a vacation."

"We're volunteers."

"Well, get your volunteer asses over to Stingray Bay. We've got a problem."

W e twisted through the posh streets of Stingray Bay. It was home to high-end luxury cars, expertly trimmed hedgerows and sprawling estates that all kind of looked the same. Nice, but uniform. This was the kind of place where everyone did their best to fit in—and it took a considerable amount of money to *fit in*.

My stomach still growled, unfulfilled. My craving for blueberry waffles would go unsatisfied.

An ambulance and the medical examiner's van were already on the scene by the time we arrived. Red and blue lights swirled atop patrol cars parked in front of the McMansion. Curious neighbors gawked and gossiped, speculating about the drama that had unfolded inside the palatial estate.

JD found a place to park. We hopped out and hustled up the walkway, past the circular drive, past a white Mercedes SUV, to the front porch. Camera flashes spilled out of the foyer as we stepped in.

Dietrich snapped photos of the deceased.

Brenda hovered over the body, examining the remains. She wore her familiar pink nitrile gloves.

The sheriff stood nearby with a grim look on his face and folded arms.

The foyer was lined with imported Italian marble with intricate inlays. There was an added design of crimson on the tile—the impact splatter of a man who'd fallen from the second story onto the hard flooring.

The foyer was larger than some smaller homes on the island. A grand central staircase spiraled up to the second floor, where a walkway led to the master bedroom and the guest bedrooms. The deceased had apparently broken through the baluster and plummeted to his death. The impact split his scalp, and ruby-red blood had oozed onto the floor. It was now dried and crusted. His lifeless brown eyes stared at the vaulted ceiling.

The deceased was late 20s, early 30s, with short brown hair, handsome features, and an athletic physique.

The broken baluster, the position of his body, and the angle of the fall led me to suspect one thing.

The fall wasn't accidental. He was pushed.

The damage to the baluster was directly across from the door to the guest room.

The door was open.

A man and a woman stood nearby, looking on with mortified faces. They were in their mid-to-late 40s. I figured them for the homeowners, judging by their attire. The Rolex on the man's wrist and the sparkly rocks on the woman's fingers were dead giveaways.

"Who's the victim?" I asked.

"Alaric Vesper," Sheriff Daniel's said.

The name didn't ring a bell.

"How long has he been this way?"

Brenda said, "Given the body temperature, I'd put the time of death between 11:00 PM to 1:00 AM."

I noticed something else odd about the situation. A small video camera sat atop a tripod in the foyer, aimed at the staircase.

"Anybody check the camera for footage?" I asked.

Daniels gave me an annoyed look. It was an obvious thing to check. "No. I've never worked a crime scene before."

I frowned at him.

"There's no recording media in the camera," he said. "No flash card, nothing. There are several cameras positioned throughout the house. All of them are the same way."

"What's that about?" I asked.

"I'll let Mr. and Mrs. Trask fill you in."

Mrs. Trask was still in a daze, but the mention of her name broke her out of her head after a moment. She cleared her throat and stepped closer.

"These are Deputies Wild and Donovan," the sheriff said, introducing us. "They're a special crimes unit."

"I'm Vivian Trask, and this is my husband, Devon."

We shook hands.

Vivian was a striking woman. She looked mid-30s rather than mid-40s. No doubt the assistance of the local plastic surgeon was utilized often. Her makeup was flawless, her teeth pearly white, and her bone structure impeccable. She had an Eastern European look to her. Her alluring blue eyes captured attention, and she carried herself with an air of sophistication. Her chocolate brown hair dangled at her shoulders.

Devon Trask looked like he could play a doctor on a soap opera. He had wavy dark hair, a square jaw lined with stubble, and touches of gray at his temples. The wrinkles around his blue eyes made him look dignified. They were a picture-perfect couple, no doubt the envy of many in Stingray Bay.

"We had hired Alaric to..." Vivian exchanged a brief glance with her husband before continuing. "You're going to think I'm crazy, but we had hired Alaric to make contact with my daughter."

JD and I looked at her with confusion.

"Make contact?"

She took a breath, steadied herself, and continued. "My daughter is no longer with us." Vivian tried to stand strong, but emotion swirled in her eyes, brimming her lids. "I don't know if you're familiar with Alaric, but he is a well-regarded medium and paranormal investigator. He's got an extremely successful *MeTube*™ channel. Millions of followers. Anyway," she said, getting back on track. "We were experiencing strange phenomena around the house."

"*You* were experiencing strange phenomena around the house," Devon clarified, clearly a skeptic.

She glared at him. "What I experienced was real!"

"I have no doubt you experienced something. What it was remains to be seen."

"I will not have you belittle my feelings on this matter."

"I'm not belittling—"

I cleared my throat. "Please continue. You were saying you hired Alaric..."

Vivian took another deep breath and tightened her jaw in frustration. "As I was saying... I experienced certain... *things*..."

"What kind of things?"

"Cold spots in the house. Doors opening and closing. Strange drafts. Hints of Lily's perfume."

"Lily was your daughter?" I asked.

Vivian nodded.

"Every single one of those things could be explained easily," Devon said. "Doors open and close all the time when the air conditioner kicks on."

Vivian's eyes burned into him. "This wasn't the air conditioner! It wasn't a draft in the house. The door closed with force. And I smelled Lily's perfume." Vivian paused for a moment, unsure. In a meek voice, she said, "And I heard voices."

Devon rolled his eyes.

Vivian scowled at him. "I heard whispers in my ear, and I swear I felt a hand on my shoulder when no one was there."

Devon stifled another eye-roll.

"I'm not crazy," Vivian assured.

He raised his hands innocently, then muttered aside, "You were crazy when I met you."

She smacked his arm.

Something told me Devon wasn't getting any action tonight.

I tried to steer things back on track. "So you hired Alaric to come in and... *investigate*?"

"Yes. That's why all the cameras are here. He live-streamed the event. He did that kind of thing all the time."

"So there may be a record of it?"

3

Vivian shook her head. "The stream cut out last night at midnight. I had been watching, but I fell asleep on the couch around 10:30 or 11:00 PM. When I woke up at 2:00 AM, the feed was out. I woke Devon, but he was unconcerned."

Devon made a face.

Vivian continued, "I wanted to come back to the house and check on things, but Devon said we should wait until morning. I was up first thing and insisted that we come back to the house, and that's when we found him."

"We didn't even have a chance to eat breakfast at the hotel," Devon said, annoyed.

"So you weren't at home at any time last night?"

They both shook their heads.

"We stayed at the Seven Seas in the Pineapple Cabana," Vivian said.

"What time did you go to the hotel?" I asked.

"We checked in around 4:00 PM, had dinner, came back to the room, and I started watching the feed."

"Was anybody in the house with Alaric last night?"

"Not that I'm aware of."

"He works alone?"

"He showed up with a cameraman yesterday afternoon, Chase Fletcher. They set up all the cameras, then Chase left. Alaric said that he liked to work alone. Too many people could spook the spirits."

JD stifled a chuckle.

"Is there anyone else that has access to the house?" I asked.

"Our son, Landon."

"Was he with you at the hotel last night?"

Vivian shook her head. "No. He stayed with a friend."

I exchanged a subtle glance with JD.

"I'd like to speak with him," I said.

She exchanged a nervous look with her husband. "I can call him."

"Please. Tell him to come to the house ASAP."

She dialed his number.

He didn't answer.

Vivian left a message. "Landon, I need you to call me back right away."

JD and I rejoined the others while Vivian kept dialing her son's number.

I asked Brenda, "Are there any other signs of trauma?"

"Just the impact," she said.

JD and I hustled up the steps to the second-floor landing. I was hoping there would be carpet and maybe there would be footprints left behind. But it was all hardwood.

We examined the broken baluster and the bedroom directly opposite. I didn't see anything unusual. Just your average guest bedroom—a dresser, a flatscreen display, a bed, two end tables. Stylish.

There was no way that Alaric fell.

I mean, maybe he stepped out of the guest bedroom, stumbled and tripped, hit the baluster, and went over. But that was a stretch.

When I returned to the first floor, Vivian said, "I spoke with Landon. He's on his way over. He should be here in a few minutes. He's at a friend's just down the street."

"Tell me exactly what happened when you returned home this morning."

The couple exchanged a glance.

Devon took the lead. "I pulled into the garage, parked the car, and we entered through the back door. I noticed right away that the power was out, which I thought was strange. So I checked the breaker. It had been tripped, so I reset it."

"A power outage would explain why the livestream went out," JD said.

I called the forensic guys and told them to dust the panel for prints.

"Did I make a mistake by turning the power back on?" Devon asked. "I didn't know Alaric was dead at that point. By the time I got back into the house, Vivian had discovered the body."

"If someone touched the breaker, we might be able to pull multiple sets of prints," I said. "We'll need an elimination set from you."

Devon nodded. "I've never been fingerprinted before. Never had a reason to."

"Don't worry," I assured. "It's painless."

Landon pushed through the front door, and his eyes widened at the sight of the dead body. "Whoa! He's really dead."

"Landon, I'd like you to meet the deputies..." Vivian began. "I'm sorry, I forgot your names."

"Wild and Donovan," I said.

"They're Special Crimes."

Landon was 17 with short dark hair, brooding brown eyes, a square jaw, and a fresh face. He had an athletic frame and stood 6'2". Not a small guy. He had a little bit of mischief to him, and I suspected the high school girls found him quite desirable. He wore a T-shirt with the logo of an indie rock band. A shark's tooth necklace hung around his collar. He'd been smoking—I could smell the cigarettes and traces of illicit herb.

"Were you at your friend's house all night last night?" I asked.

"Yeah, why?"

"Did you come back to the house at any time?"

He shook his head.

"Who did you stay with?"

"Jason."

"I'll need his contact information," I said.

His eyes flicked to his parents, then back to me. "What for?"

"Just routine."

He nodded and shrugged. "Okay."

"What did you guys do last night?" I asked.

He shrugged again. "Just hung out."

"Can you be more specific?"

"You know, we just chilled. Jason had a few people over."

"Did you have a party?" Vivian asked, concerned.

"No, we didn't have a party," he said, annoyed. "Just a few people came over."

"Who?"

"Some girls. What's the big deal?"

"Were Jason's parents home?"

"Yeah, totally." He lied.

Her eyes narrowed with suspicion. "What girls?"

"Some girls from school. Can we talk about this later?"

"Did the girls spend the night at Jason's?"

"No."

"You better be careful," Vivian said. "If you knock some girl up, that's gonna change your life."

"Mom!"

I steered things back on track. "Had you met Alaric prior to yesterday?"

"No. I knew who he was. I'd seen his videos before."

"Did you watch any of the livestream last night?" I asked.

4

"Here and there," Landon said. "It was pretty boring. Nothing really happened. At least, not from what I saw. There was no *strange phenomenon*," he said, mocking his mother.

Vivian glared at him.

"I take it you haven't experienced any of this paranormal activity?"

"Not really. I mean, I'll have dreams about my sister every now and then. They seem real. One time, I woke up and felt like there was a presence in the room. But it was just a dream."

"Lily was clearly trying to communicate with you," Vivian said.

"Look, she's dead. She killed herself. She's not coming back. She's not trying to talk to us. She's gone. And newsflash, there's nothing after this. It's all bullshit."

Vivian stiffened, and her face tensed—a mix of rage and sadness. Her eyes brimmed. "You will not speak to me like that in this house!" Vivian couldn't hold the emotions back, and she broke down into sobs. She cried, "I just want to know why. She had everything. We loved her so much."

Landon shared a glance with his father. "Are we done here? Can I go?"

"That's all for now," I said.

"Can I go to my room?"

"The whole house is a crime scene."

He spun around and marched out the door. "I'm going back to Jason's."

His sister's death had affected him, and he was processing it through anger. He disconnected. That was my take, anyway.

Devon put his arm around his wife and tried to comfort her as she sobbed.

"I know this is a delicate subject, but did your daughter leave any type of note?" I asked.

Devon shook his head. "Her boyfriend broke up with her and left town. She was devastated. I tried to tell her that she was young and there were plenty of opportunities to meet her soulmate. I thought she was doing okay, then..." He shook his head.

"Did it happen in this house?"

Devon nodded.

"When did this happen?"

"Not even a month ago."

It was still fresh. Even after 20 years, that kind of thing remains fresh.

I exchanged information with the Trasks, then JD and I looked around the property.

There were no signs of forced entry.

We left the scene and stepped outside.

More curious neighbors had gathered.

Paris Delaney and her news crew accosted us. The camera lens pushed in, and a sound guy angled a fluffy boom microphone overhead. The ambitious blonde was never far from a tragedy. "Deputy Wild, what can you tell us?"

I gave her an overview of the situation. "If anyone saw anything suspicious, please contact the Coconut County Sheriff's Department."

We stepped out of frame and walked back to the Porsche. JD slid behind the wheel and cranked up the engine. I climbed into the passenger seat and pulled my phone from my pocket.

"What do you think about all that?" JD asked.

"I think somebody pushed him over the railing."

"You buy into the other stuff?"

I gave him a look.

I was a skeptic by nature, but having had a near-death experience myself, I had complex views on the subject. I knew one thing for certain—I'd been given a second chance, and I was going to do my best to make the most of it.

Jack pulled away from the curb, making his way through the emergency vehicles. His long blond hair fluttered in the breeze, and the air swirled about the cabin.

I dialed Isabella, my handler at Cobra Company. The clandestine agency had vast intelligence resources. Isabella had all kinds of technology at her disposal. Her methods weren't always legal, and we couldn't use the information she gave us in a court of law, but she could often shed light on things.

We had pretty much moved past our *quid pro quo* status. But I suspected somewhere down the line she was going to ask for a big favor.

"What kind of trouble are you in today?"

"No trouble, just a bizarre death."

"Define bizarre?"

I gave her an overview of the situation and asked her to see if she could identify any cellular devices that pinged the tower from the mansion at the time of Alaric's death.

"I'll see what I can find. Sounds spooky."

"It sounds like somebody didn't like Alaric Vesper."

"I'm sure you'll get to the bottom of it."

"I appreciate the confidence."

We headed back to the station, filled out after-action reports in the conference room under the pale fluorescent lights, typing away on iPads.

The place was plastered with Halloween decor, thanks to Denise. Cutouts of black cats, ghouls, and ghosts hung on the walls. Orange and black ribbons streamed through hallways. The spooky season was upon us.

Denise poked her head into the conference room. The delicious redhead was always a refreshing sight. "Ran background on the deceased. Alaric Vesper lived on Sawgrass Lane with his wife. I already did the notification, but I told her you two would stop by to speak with her." She paused. "Did you watch that guy's show?"

We shook our heads.

"I'd seen a few episodes before." Denise shrugged, not terribly enthused. "It was... *interesting*."

"Did he ever find any ghosts?" I asked in a doubtful tone.

"That's debatable. I mean, he'd act like he was communicating with spirits from beyond, but who really knows? He could have been faking it."

I found Alaric's MeTube channel. We all huddled around the iPad as I replayed the livestream from last night. Multiple cameras were positioned throughout the house, and the software would automatically cut to the camera that detected motion. The lights were off in the house except for a solitary candle that Alaric kept with him as he roamed through the house, calling out to the spirits, letting them know that he was a friend.

Alaric moved up the stairs and down the hall. He stepped into Lily's room, which remained just as she'd left it. The luxury deco-style bedroom was elegant yet cozy. A plush gray velvet Chesterfield bed was the centerpiece. A white furry comforter provided contrast. The wall against the headboard was covered in shimmering gray and silver wallpaper. The other walls were white. Mirrored nightstands flanked the bed, and modern white shelving contained luxury purses and other fashion items. A glass desk and a makeup table with mirrored accents complemented the nightstands. White furry throw rugs matched the comforter. A marvelous chandelier hung overhead, and a cozy gray velvet couch provided a place to relax or read a book.

Alaric sat on the bed, closed his eyes, and took a deep breath. "Lily, if you're here, your mother has a message for you. Please communicate with me. She desperately needs to hear from you."

5

Alaric had a small spirit box, which was basically a transistor radio that swept through the frequencies. It was mostly garbled static, but every now and then, you could hear something—something that could be construed as a word or phrase.

In my view, it was kind of like a Rorschach test. It was open to interpretation, and oftentimes you could hear what you wanted to hear in the garbled mess of static.

"Lily, are you here?" Alaric asked again.

A garbled response came out of the spirit box, "Yes."

Alaric repeated the answer for the audience, "Yes."

If you were watching the livestream late at night in a darkened room, it might be a little spooky. A tingle might run down your spine, and the hairs on the back of your neck might stand up. Under the harsh light of the conference room, we all watched with skepticism.

Alaric smiled. "Thank you for speaking with me. Your mother misses you very much."

The room was silent for a moment.

"Lily, are you still there?"

More static.

Finally, "I'm not Lily."

We all exchanged curious looks.

JD said, "Did you hear that?"

"I don't know what I heard. I heard noise on a random radio frequency."

"I don't know," Denise said. "I think I heard it."

JD shook his head dismissively.

"Who are you?" Alaric asked.

There was no response.

"If you're still here, flicker the candle."

Alaric held steady, and an instant later, the candlelight flickered for a moment, illuminating his face in a spooky glow.

Then it went out.

The grainy green glow of the night vision kept the room barely visible.

I wasn't buying into the whole thing. He could have easily manipulated the candle. An exhale could make it flicker.

"This is kind of creepy," Denise said.

"Then you're going to love the job I have for you," I said.

She gave me a look, knowing where I was going. "You want me to watch the livestream until it cuts out."

I smiled. "Please?"

"What's in it for me?"

"It's your job."

"You're not the boss of me."

I sighed. "What do you want?"

She smiled. "I'll think of something."

"I'm sure you will. How about dinner and drinks?"

She laughed. "That would be a treat for you."

I scoffed. "I don't know about that. I mean, I guess I could suffer through it."

She sneered at me playfully, then sauntered out of the conference room.

"You need to get on that," JD muttered. "Departmental rules be damned."

I left the station and headed over to Sawgrass to speak with Nina Vesper. The couple lived in a quaint bungalow with a white picket fence, tall palms, and a colorful flower garden. The home had mint green siding with white trim and a small veranda. A brick walkway led to the front porch.

Paranormal investigations must pay well.

It wasn't Stingray Bay, but it was a nice place.

I banged on the front door, and Nina answered a moment later. She had flowing brown hair that hung past her shoulders and dark eyes. Tan skin and a petite figure. She was an attractive woman.

I flashed my badge and made introductions. "I'm sorry for your loss."

She nodded. Nina looked more stunned than upset. Understandable. It often took time for reality to hit in situations like these.

"I know this is a difficult time, but we just have a few questions for you."

She nodded again and stepped aside. "Please, come in."

She led us through the foyer into the living room. It was a cozy little place with bleached hardwoods, light furniture, tropical accents, and lemongrass walls. French doors opened to a small patio area with wrought-iron chairs and a table with an umbrella. The area was enclosed by a high fence lined with flower gardens. A nice space to relax in the evening and entertain guests.

She offered us a seat on the sofa, and we obliged.

"Can I get you anything to drink?"

"No, thank you," I said.

She took a chair catty-corner. "The deputy I spoke with on the phone said Alaric fell?"

She was uncertain and confused.

"He plummeted from the second story," I said. "Whether he fell or was pushed, we can't be certain at this time."

Her brow lifted, and her eyes rounded. "Pushed?"

"Like I said, we're not sure."

Her face crinkled with confusion. "I don't understand. Who would have pushed him?"

"Did Alaric have any enemies?"

She thought for a moment. "Not that I know of." She paused. "Well, I mean, he had some issues with people."

I exchanged a glance with JD.

"Can you elaborate?" JD asked.

"Well, he was having trouble with a client," Nina said.

"What kind of trouble?" I asked.

"The client was unhappy with the services provided. He wanted a refund of his money, but Alaric wouldn't do it. This person called the house on several occasions. He came by once, making threats. He accused Alaric of scamming him."

"Did he?"

Nina gave me a sharp look. "I don't know. Who's really to say?"

"Seems like Alaric had built quite a following online."

She nodded. "People can't get enough of this kind of thing. I mean, we all want to believe that there's something more, right? Something beyond. Something unseen."

"Some people might see that as praying on the hopes and fears of desperate people wanting to communicate with deceased loved ones."

"You're a skeptic," she said.

"Are you a believer?"

6

Nina hesitated for a moment. "I believe there are many things that we don't know about The Universe. Things we can't explain. Does that mean they don't exist?"

I shrugged.

"I can't tell you what Alaric saw or felt or who he communicated with, if anyone at all. Was it all an elaborate hoax driven solely by profit? Did he have real paranormal experiences? Was it all just a figment of his imagination? I don't know the answers to those questions, and it seems irrelevant now."

"Have you ever experienced the paranormal?"

"No. But then again, I'm not sensitive to it. Some people are, some people aren't, I suppose."

"How was your relationship with Alaric?" I asked.

Her alluring eyes stared at me for a moment, trying to discern where I was going. "Less-than-perfect, but what marriage is perfect?"

"Can you tell me what *less-than-perfect* means?"

She hesitated a moment. "Alaric could be really sweet, or he could be a bastard. You never really knew what you were going to get. He had a short fuse and could blow up over the smallest things."

"Was he ever abusive?"

She sighed. "I guess there's no harm in sharing my dirty laundry now. He's not here to retaliate. So, yes." Her eyes fell to her lap. "He could be quite temperamental."

"Was the abuse physical?"

"Physical, verbal, you name it."

"Why did you stay?"

She paused. "I don't know. Emotions are complicated things, aren't they?"

I nodded. "Can you tell me where you were last night?"

Her eyes narrowed as they flicked to me again. "I'm a suspect, aren't I?"

"Spouses always are."

"Especially ones that tell you they were in an abusive marriage," she said. Nina was no dummy.

I nodded again.

"You'll probably want to know that I'm the beneficiary of a large life insurance policy."

"That is helpful information."

She confronted this head-on. The seductive brunette clearly had an ace up her sleeve.

Nina leaned forward, resting her elbows on her knees. "Rest assured, gentlemen. I did not kill my husband." An almost imperceptible smile tugged her plump lips. "I was here all night last night."

"Can anyone else verify that?"

"Yes. Tristan Davis was here with me. You can speak to him if you'd like."

"Your lover?"

"At the moment," she said with a seductive eyebrow. "Lord knows Alaric had his conquests. Why shouldn't I have mine?"

"So he was going outside the marriage?"

"He was always going outside of our relationship. It took me a while to realize that, but two can play that game."

"You weren't concerned about having your lover stay here overnight?"

"When Alaric was working, it was easy to know where he was."

"The livestream went out around midnight."

"I wasn't watching."

"What were you doing?"

She smirked again. "You want a detailed description?"

She was almost flirting. *Almost.*

"I'll need contact information for Tristan," I said. "As well as the disgruntled client that made threats."

"Jim Gallagher," Nina said. "You might also want to look into Thaddeus Crane."

"Who's that?"

"Alaric's former business partner."

She had my curiosity.

"They had a falling out," she continued.

"Over what?"

"Alaric wanted to do his own thing. They had different ideas about how to develop the brand. Alaric became very successful, Thaddeus did not. Of course, he tried to mimic Alaric's success with his own channel, but he just didn't have a knack for capturing attention like Alaric did."

"Did he ever make threats?"

"Thaddeus got Alaric into the game. Helped him develop his skill. I think he felt betrayed when Alaric left."

After she gave me their contact information, we offered our condolences once again and said our goodbyes. JD and I left the house and strolled the walkway back toward the Porsche.

"You know her boyfriend is going to cover for her," JD said.

"Of course. What else would he do?"

"She's certainly got a motive, and she's not shy about it. You know she's on the phone with her lover right now."

"I would expect nothing less."

We headed back to Diver Down and grabbed lunch at the bar. Blueberry waffles would have to wait.

Teagan greeted us with a cheery smile, her bikini top jiggling in hypnotic ways. The teal-eyed beauty could uplift anyone's spirits. "How is your day going?"

"Have you seen the news?"

She nodded.

"That's how it's going," I said. "I have a proposition for you."

She looked at me with concern. "Is this the kind of proposition I might like?"

"It's right up your alley."

"No!" she said, knowing exactly where this was going.

"You haven't even heard what I have to say."

"I know what you're going to say. Alaric Vesper was a psychic medium. You want me to visit the house where he died and use my psychic ability to connect with the spirits of the departed. I am here to tell you not only no, but hell no! Have you lost your ever-loving mind?"

"I think he lost that a long time ago," JD muttered.

"What could it hurt?" I asked.

Teagan scoffed. "Do you want me to give you a list? First... Every now and then I get vibes about things or a vision of something. That is entirely different from channeling the energy of the dead. Second... Do you remember what happened the last time I helped you with a case?"

I frowned. It got ugly.

Teagan's supposed psychic powers came and went, and she was always hesitant to use them. Every time she did, something bad happened. I don't know if I believed in the whole thing, but at this point, the situation was so outrageous, what could it hurt?

She was about to tell me.

"And lastly, there is no way that I'm going to go into some haunted mansion and open up some portal to the beyond. Who knows what's on the other side? You don't know who you're talking to. You don't know what their intentions are. You don't know if they're going to follow you home and start haunting you. Sorry, honey, but there ain't enough money in the world."

I raised my hands in surrender. "It was just a thought."

"Besides, my gift has vanished at the moment. And I hope it stays gone forever."

"Forget I asked."

"I will."

In a sad, pathetic voice, I said, "I guess we'll just have to go down to the strip and find some charlatan to help us out."

She shifted onto one hip, tilted her head, and squinted her eyes. "Since when do you even buy into that kind of thing?"

"I don't. I'm just keeping an open mind."

She rolled her eyes. "The charlatans on the strip are not going to work. You know as well as I do, those palm readers are hustlers. If you really want to find someone to help you with the case, I can give you a name."

I lifted a curious brow. "Who?"

7

"I don't know if she will do this kind of thing, but it's worth a shot," Teagan said.

"Is she a friend of yours?"

"An acquaintance. Her name is Prim Sterling."

"Is she cute?" JD asked.

Teagan's eyes narrowed at me. "No. She's 90 years old, and I don't think you want to see her in a bikini."

Jack frowned. "Thanks for the visual."

"Tell her I sent you. I don't think she's real big on cops, but you two aren't your average cops." Then she added, "And behave. Don't harass her."

"When have we ever harassed anyone?" JD asked.

I said, "What's her issue with cops?"

"You'll have to ask her. I'm not psychic," she snarked.

I sneered at her playfully.

She gave me Prim's contact information, then took our order.

JD went with the shrimp wrap with pineapple salsa, and I had the chicken quesadillas with Monterey Jack, caramelized onions, sour cream, and guacamole.

If anything, Prim might be able to give us a little insight into the world of the paranormal. She might have known Alaric and Thaddeus and could offer a valuable perspective. If not, I was always open to meeting new people. There was a lot to be learned from someone in their 90s—mainly, how to make it that long. At the rate we were going, JD and I didn't have to worry about old age.

We chowed down, and I did a little research online. I found some interesting information about Thaddeus Crane.

"Hey," Teagan said to me privately in a soft voice. "So, I need to talk to you about something."

"What's up?" I asked with trepidation.

"Hey, can I get another beer?" a customer shouted.

"Later, when it's not so busy," Teagan whispered to me.

"Ok."

She grabbed a longneck from a tub of ice, drew a bottle opener from her back pocket like a gunslinger, and popped the top with a hiss. She served the patron with a smile.

I got the idea she was nervous about bringing up the discussion, whatever it was.

After lunch, we headed across the island to catch up with Thaddeus. He lived in a crappy little apartment on the edge of Jamaica Village, which wasn't the greatest part of town. It was a stark contrast from Alaric's cozy little cottage.

Jack found a place to park on the street in front of the cinderblock building that was painted a dull brown. It had water stains around the base where rain had kicked up mud and debris. The lawn was patchy and in need of trimming. A few tall palms presided overhead. The rectangular structure housed eight units—four up, four down.

The narrow street was lined with vehicles in various conditions—lots of faded paint and dented quarter panels. It wasn't unusual for a larger vehicle to clip a side mirror or scrape a body panel.

JD gave a cautious glance around as we left the vehicle behind and strolled the walkway to unit #104. A brilliant Porsche with the top down around here was asking for trouble.

I put a heavy fist against the door and shouted, "Coconut County."

The TV in the living room filtered through the door. Commotion rumbled inside, and footsteps approached. The peephole flickered as Thaddeus peered through. He opened a moment later.

His narrow blue eyes darted between the two of us. He was a rather flamboyant man with wavy brown hair that hung past his ears, a trimmed mustache, and long sideburns that extended to his jawline. He had an aristocratic quality about him, despite living in near poverty. I figured him for early 30s. He wore a paisley vest, slacks, and an ascot scarf around his neck. "I suppose you're here about Alaric Vesper?"

"What would give you that idea?" I asked.

"I watch the news. Someone killed him. I'm his former business partner, and it's no secret that we had our disagreements."

"Care to elaborate on those disagreements?"

"It's simple, really. I brought him into this world. I taught him everything he knew, and how did he repay me? By stabbing me in the back."

"How so?"

"It's obvious, but I can spell it out for you, if you insist," he said in a snooty tone.

My expression urged him to continue.

"We had a non-compete agreement. Alaric was prohibited from engaging in any paranormal investigative services for three years after his departure. He took the secrets that I taught him, ways of communicating with the departed, my techniques. He disparaged my business and pilfered my cameraman."

"Chase Fletcher," I said for confirmation.

Thaddeus nodded.

"Sounds like you had a motive to kill the man."

"You won't catch me shedding a tear over his loss."

"Where were you last night?"

"I was here."

"By yourself?"

"Unfortunately."

"How's business?" I asked.

"Does it look like business is great? Would I be living in this dump if I could afford anything else? Alaric was like a vacuum. His popularity sucked up all the local jobs. People flocked to him for their paranormal needs." His face tightened with disdain. "Now nobody is calling me to exorcize demons from their home, contact a deceased loved one, or help them with matters of the heart."

"Maybe you should market your services better," I suggested.

His eyes narrowed at me. "I believe that if you offer a quality product and service, people will come to you."

"Do you offer a quality product and service?"

People obviously weren't flocking to him.

He took offense. "Indeed, I do. I am the best on the island, if I do say so myself."

Thaddeus certainly wasn't modest.

"That's not what the reviews say."

His cheeks flushed, and his jaw tightened. "A smear campaign by my rival to diminish my reputation. I can assure you, I am as authentic as they come."

"Was Alaric authentic?"

"When we were working together, Alaric couldn't communicate with the living, much less the dead."

"So you two were scamming people?"

8

T had's cheeks reddened again, and the veins in his forehead pulsed. "I have never scammed anyone in my entire life. I can't speak for Alaric Vesper."

I wasn't entirely sure about that.

"Are you sure you didn't pay him a visit last night at the Trask mansion and push him over the railing?"

He forced a smile. "As appealing as that sounds, sadly, I did not. But I envy the person who did. The sense of satisfaction must be immense." His smile widened. "Now, if you'll excuse me, gentlemen, I have urgent business to attend to."

He had no business.

We left and headed back to the Porsche. It was still in one piece, just as we'd left it, which was something to be thankful for, especially in this neighborhood. It wasn't terrible here, but three or four blocks over, and you were taking your life in your hands.

We hopped into the car, and JD pulled away from the curb. "What do you make of that guy?"

"A solid motive, no alibi, and plenty of pent-up animosity."

"That can be a potent combination."

We headed across the island to catch up with Chase Fletcher.

We found him at the Mariner's Wharf apartments, which weren't anywhere near the wharf. The units had a rustic cottage style. Weathered wood buildings with white trim and traditional pane windows, with a few round portholes here and there. Oak doors and stone pathways. A hand-crafted sign displayed the name, and lush palms guarded the grounds.

I banged on the door to unit B102.

Chase answered a moment later. He was in his early 20s with medium-length shaggy blonde hair, brown eyes, and chiseled features. He had a surfer vibe and a laid-back demeanor.

I flashed my badge.

"I guess you're here about Alaric?"

I nodded.

"What happened?"

He was asking the right questions. I get suspicious when people aren't curious as to the manner of death.

I gave him a brief overview.

"I hadn't heard from him today, which was unusual after a gig. Then I got online and read about it." He shook his head in disbelief. "I don't know how that could have happened."

"You set up the cameras last night, right?" I asked.

"Yeah."

"What time did you leave the house?"

"I met him over there in the early evening after I got off work. I placed the cameras where he wanted, and he told me he'd call in the morning. I usually pick up the gear in the morning, but I never heard from him. I called a few times, then checked the feed. I thought it was weird he didn't call when it went out."

"You didn't watch last night?"

He shook his head like it was a dumb question. "No. Why would I? It's pretty boring if you ask me. It's just Alaric running around, pretending like he's talking to ghosts. I don't see the attraction, personally. He usually calls if there's a problem, but I never heard from him last night. Obviously, now I know why."

"Is it your equipment?"

"Yeah. Is it still at the house?"

"No, it's in evidence right now."

He lifted a surprised brow. "I'll get it back, right?"

"Eventually."

"Bro, I need that gear. It's how I make a living."

"You do this for anybody else?"

"I work at Coconut Productions, but I do video for a few influencers on the side. Odd jobs here and there. Sometimes I'll shoot music videos, small commercials. Whatever."

The wheels turned behind JD's eyes. "You film live bands?"

"Sure. Why not?"

I steered things back on track. "We'll get the gear back to you as soon as possible. There was something curious about the cameras. All the recording media was removed," I said.

Confusion wrinkled Chase's face. "All the SD cards are gone? Where are they?"

I shrugged. "I think whoever killed Alaric took the evidence."

"You really think he was killed?"

"I don't believe a ghost pushed him over the railing."

"Yeah, I read some of those comments online. Ridiculous."

"So, you're a skeptic?"

"I just set up the cameras, bro."

"You ever seen anything strange while working with Alaric?"

"I'm never there. Like I said, I set up and leave. It's a great gig. I collect the footage and edit it down to shorter content after the livestream."

"Did Alaric pay well?"

Chase shook his head. "Not really. But it was an easy gig."

"Did you get along?"

"Yeah, we got along great. Why?"

"Just curious. Do you know Jim Gallagher?"

His brow knitted as he thought about it. "That's the guy that was pissed off at Alaric."

I nodded. "You know much about that?"

"Not really. I remember setting up the cameras at that guy's house. If I recall, Alaric did a lot of work for that guy. I don't think he was too happy with the results."

"What was he hoping to accomplish?"

"He wanted Alaric to get in touch with his departed grandfather. Shocker. It didn't happen."

"But Alaric strung him along," I theorized.

Chase shrugged. "I'm not going to say one way or the other. Put it to you this way, I wouldn't spend that kind of money without tangible results."

"Seems like that's what Jim Gallagher is pissed off about."

Chase shrugged again. "You know what they say about suckers and their money."

"Can you think of anybody else who had a beef with Alaric?"

"You think somebody snuck into the mansion and pushed him over the railing?"

"I don't think he fell."

Chase thought about it for a moment. "You're aware of what happened a few months ago, aren't you?"

My eyes filled with curiosity.

9

"What happened a few months ago?" I asked.

Chase continued, "Stacy Buchanan died."

I exchanged a look with JD. "Who's Stacy Buchanan?"

"Hot little number. 22. Real smoke show."

"Alaric was seeing her?" I speculated.

He nodded. "They were out diving one of the shipwrecks. Regulator failed or something like that. Stacy panicked. She drowned. At least, that's the way I heard it. Don't ask me. I wasn't there. Her family blames Alaric. Filed a wrongful death suit. I remember Alaric telling me about Stacy's dad threatening him."

"Did Alaric's wife know about his affair with Stacy Buchanan?"

"I think she stopped giving a shit what he did, honestly."

"You know what happened to the wrongful death suit?"

"I don't know. He didn't talk about it much after it happened. Her family was trying to say that Alaric was negligent and didn't properly maintain the equipment. But, you know... shit breaks. I don't see how that's his fault."

"Where did you say you were last night?"

"I went over to my girlfriend's apartment."

"I'll need her contact information," I said.

"Why? You want to verify my alibi?"

"Yep."

He laughed. "Why would I kill the guy I worked for?"

"Maybe there's something you're not telling us."

He chuckled again. "I think I pretty much told you everything, but I'll give you Josie's number."

He texted me her contact info, and I gave him a card.

"Get in touch if you can think of anything else," I said.

"Sure thing."

We left and walked back to the car.

"I'm not getting killer vibes from that guy."

"Neither am I, but you never know."

I pulled out my phone and dialed Josie Clark. She confirmed that she spent the evening with Chase. I didn't have any real reason to doubt her.

My next call was to Denise. I asked her to pull information on Stacy Buchanan as we drove across the island to find Jim Gallagher. I'd find out soon that Jim was quite the character.

The keyboard clacked as Denise stroked the keys. "Brenda ruled Stacy's death accidental. In her report, she goes on to say that the regulator Stacy was using experienced a first-stage failure, sealing off the airflow."

"That's unusual," I said.

"According to the report, this particular regulator had an automatic closer designed to prevent water from infiltrating the first stage. In his statement, Alaric said they were diving the wreck, and he lost sight of Stacy inside the ship. The regulator failed, and she panicked and drowned before she could escape the wreckage. He found her, brought her to the surface, and attempted CPR, to no avail."

"What about the lawsuit?" I asked.

"It looks like Stacy's parents have a civil suit against the manufacturer. A product safety notice was posted on the website about the device, urging consumers to routinely check their units. The case against Alaric was dismissed. The judge said he couldn't reasonably be expected to know about the regulator's design failure, therefore, wasn't liable. The litigation against the manufacturer is ongoing." Denise paused. "I can understand being angry, but it doesn't sound like it was Alaric's fault."

"Unless he tampered with the regulator," I said.

"Why kill his mistress?"

"Maybe she was putting pressure on him."

"To leave his wife?"

"Who knows?"

"Breaking it off seems easier than murder," Denise said.

"Maybe it was just an accident. But I like to keep an open mind."

"And you think Stacy's parents took revenge?"

"It's worth looking into."

Her fingers tapped the keys again. "Miles Buchanan. I'll text you his info."

"Much appreciated."

I ended the call, and my phone buzzed with a text from Denise as we pulled into Jim Gallagher's residence. He'd recently inherited his grandfather's house and was living at 1520 Driftwood Drive. It was a nice little bungalow, not too far from the beach. We parked at the curb, hopped out, and pushed through the white picket fence. A red brick walkway led up to a small veranda. I put a fist against the door, and it wasn't long before the floorboards creaked as Jim stepped into the foyer.

The house had sky-blue siding with white trim and a red door. Tall palms towered overhead, and the yard was filled with lush foliage—though it didn't look like he'd been keeping it up too well since he'd taken over. An American flag hung from a column on the veranda.

Jim pulled open the door and gave us a curious look. "What do you want?"

He was a short, round man in his early 50s that liked his junk food. A scraggly grayish-brown beard rimmed his face. He didn't have a jawline—it disappeared amid the extra chin. He had short brown hair peppered with speckles of gray, narrow eyes, and square glasses. He wore a T-shirt, cargo shorts, and looked like he was enjoying a life of leisure.

I flashed my badge and made introductions. "I understand you're a former client of Alaric Vesper."

His face soured at the name. "Fuck that guy!"

"Tell us how you really feel?" JD muttered.

"I feel like that prick owes me money, and he died before he could give it to me."

"Why does he owe you money?"

"Because he ripped me off."

"You were unhappy with his services?" I asked.

"You're goddamn right," he said, growing more and more agitated.

"Why did you hire him?"

He hesitated. "I don't have to tell you."

"We're just here to talk."

"Fuck you."

I looked at JD, then back to Jim. "No need to get hostile."

"I'm not hostile. Who's hostile?"

Jim was kind of kooky.

"It's my understanding you hired Alaric to make contact with your grandfather."

"Who told you that?"

"What was the problem?" I asked, ignoring his question.

"The problem is my grandfather is dead. And I need to talk to him."

"What about?"

"None of your damn business."

"So you hired Alaric to make contact. What happened?"

Jim sighed. "I paid that no-good son-of-a-bitch $50,000. He promised me he could communicate with my grandfather and find out what I needed to know."

"What do you need to know?"

"What does it matter to you?"

"This is a nice place you got here," I said, changing the subject.

"No shit."

"So Alaric took your money but didn't provide results."

"Oh, I think he got results. Just not for me."

"What do you mean?"

His mouth tightened, and his eyes shifted between the two of us. "Is this conversation confidential?"

"Absolutely."

Conversations with cops are *never* confidential.

He looked around to make sure no one was within earshot, then leaned in and spoke in a hushed tone. "You can't say a word about this to anybody."

"Mums the word," I said with a pantomime.

10

"The lost treasure of Jacques De La Fontaine," Jim said.

"What about it?" I asked.

We'd been searching for the lost treasure forever. So had everyone else in the area. It was an obsession with Jack.

We thought we had found the lost pirate ship, the *Black Rose*, but it turned out to be the *Royal Revenge*.

It wasn't a bad consolation prize.

The bronze cannons alone were worth a large fortune, and there was more gold aboard the ship than we could spend in a lifetime. Demi De Luca was in charge of the salvage operation. Her take was 50%. She was doing a damn good job, but it was a painstaking process to get those cannons up from the seafloor and restore them.

Jack had this crazy idea about building an exact replica of the Royal Revenge and turning it into a floating museum. That was proving more difficult than anticipated, and he'd been talking with Logan Chase about acquiring the pirate ship used in the *Curse of the Caribbean*. But the studio had other plans. At the end of the trilogy, which had yet to be completed, the director wanted to blow the ship up in a climactic battle. No CGI. All practical effects. Logan had given us the bad news when he called. We'd have to find a pirate ship elsewhere or have one constructed.

Finding the *Royal Revenge* had quenched our treasure-hunting thirsts for the time being, but the allure of Jacques De La Fontaine was too hard to pass up. It was the stuff of legend. Rumor had it bits and pieces of the treasure were strewn up and down the coastline from the wreckage. Others said that was all nonsense and that the infamous French pirate had buried it on one of the islands. Others said it didn't exist at all. It was hard to sort fact from fiction. Even the personal memoir of Jacques De La Fontaine was loaded with misdirection.

"My grandfather found it," Jim said with awe and wonder.

"He found the treasure?" I asked, skeptical.

"Yes. He died before he could tell me where it was."

"And you hired Alaric to talk to your grandfather and find out where it is."

"You catch on quick. I'm convinced he learned the location and is keeping the treasure for himself."

"That's why you killed him?"

His face twisted. "What!?"

"Sounds like a hell of a motive to me?"

"Why would I kill the guy when he knows where the treasure is? I wouldn't do that." He muttered aside, starting in a hushed tone that grew with rage, "I'd kidnap the guy and torture him until he told me what I wanted to know. I'd threaten to cut his balls off. Pull his fingernails out. Take a ball peen hammer to his toes." His face was red and angry by now. "That fucker would tell me, alright. That's what I would do. Now that he's dead, I'll never find that treasure."

He had a point.

"Where were you last night?"

"I was at Forbidden Fruit."

Something told me that Jim Gallagher was burning through his inheritance as fast as humanly possible. "What time?"

"I don't know. I went to the club around 10:00 PM. Stayed there till close. Brought a couple girls back to the house. Kicked them out this morning."

"You brought a couple girls back to the house?" I asked, skeptical. Jim didn't strike me as a lady-killer.

"What? You think I can't pull stripper ass?"

I raised my hands in surrender.

"Chicks dig me. They don't want pretty boys. They want a man of style and substance."

"You got that to spare," I said, trying not to sound too sarcastic.

His eyes narrowed, unsure if I was messing with him.

"Who are the two girls you were with?"

"Crystal and Gigi."

"And they'll be able to confirm your story?"

"Absolutely."

I gave him my card and told him we'd be in touch.

We returned to the Porsche.

"Sounds like we might need to make a trip to Forbidden Fruit," JD said with a sparkle in his eyes.

11

___

Spotlights slashed the hazy air, and sultry pop music pumped through massive speakers.

"Serenity, stage two. Serenity, stage two," the DJ said in a smooth, low voice.

Delightful beauties pranced the stage in stiletto heels, tantalizing the crowd with mesmerizing peaks and supple assets. Shimmering thighs and toned calves. Heartbreaks and dreams.

The manager, Jacko, leaned against the bar, surveying his domain. He flashed a smile and waved us over when he spotted us. Forbidden Fruit was the premiere strip club on the island.

Jacko was an old-school New Yorker, and he greeted us with a firm handshake and a smile. "You got that look in your eyes. This is business. I can tell."

At this point, we were regulars in the club—strictly for investigative purposes, of course.

Looking for Gigi and Crystal.

"I don't think they're in today," Jacko said, surveying the floor. "I'm sure I can find you something else to suit your fancy."

"You have contact information for them?"

"I should have that in my phone."

He pulled out his device and thumbed through the contact list, then sent the information to me.

"Why don't you stay, have a round of drinks on the house?"

It was a tempting offer.

"We're in the middle of an investigation," I said.

"Come on. One drink?"

I knew that one drink in this place turned into five in a heartbeat.

"You never know, you might find true love," Jacko sang.

"Or true lust."

Jacko smiled.

"Next time."

"You're a better man than I."

"Yeah, but I'm not," JD said. "Fire up a round."

Jacko smiled. "That's the spirit."

"One drink," I muttered to him. "We've got things to accomplish."

In the spirit of the season, there were plenty of girls in—or out of—costume. Sultry vampires, sexy cat girls, steamy nurses. Tight leather and fishnets. High heels and lacy bras.

We found an empty table not far from the main stage and took a seat. Jacko sent over a waitress with our drinks, and two delightful beauties joined us for a good *conversation*.

It didn't take much persuasion for tops to come off and booties to shake. We sipped the whiskey and enjoyed the ladies' delights. It would have been easy to shirk our responsibilities and pick up the investigation tomorrow, but somehow I managed to steer things back on track after one —or possibly three—dances.

This was all Jacko's fault.

We were just killing time to see if Crystal or Gigi showed up. That was as good an excuse as any.

The sun squinted my eyes as I stepped onto the sidewalk. The dull beat of the bass drum filtered out of the club.

Oyster Avenue was decked out with orange and black in preparation for Halloween. Banners crossed the street with spooky lettering. Pennants hung from lamp-posts. Storefronts were decorated with black cats, spiderwebs, coffins, classic vampires, ghosts, and ghouls.

Halloween was a big deal on the strip. Every year, thousands of revelers flocked to the boulevard dressed in outrageous costumes.

It was the place to be.

The horror convention at The Hyton brought thousands and thousands of fans from across the nation. The spooky season on the island was the most magical time of the year. There were parties and rituals. Wild Fury was set to take the main stage on the strip, playing a free open-air concert at the *Spooky Festival*.

JD frowned at me and muttered. "We could have stayed for one more."

I pulled my phone from my pocket and called Crystal. It went to voicemail, so I left a message, then dialed Gigi.

She didn't pick up either.

We walked back to the car and set out to find Miles Buchanan, Stacy's father.

12

M iles Buchanan lived in the upscale neighborhood of *Whispering Heights*. Not Stingray Bay, but not too shabby. The house was sleek and modern but not sterile. Sharp, angular lines met graceful curves. Large window walls allowed copious amounts of light to flood into the space. The yard was a lush oasis of tropical plants, flowers, and other foliage. Majestic palms stood guard, dancing with the gentle sea breeze. The home backed up to a private white sand beach where emerald and sapphire waves crashed the shore.

The wrongful death suits weren't about money. From the looks of things, Miles Buchanan had more than enough of it. They were about some form of justice. But nothing would bring back Stacy.

JD parked the Porsche at the curb, and we hustled up the walkway to the front porch. I rang the video doorbell, and a moment later, a voice crackled through the speaker.

I displayed my badge to the lens and made introductions. "We'd like to ask you a few questions."

The line crackled. Miles remained silent for a moment. Finally, "What's this about?"

I was pretty sure he knew damn good and well what this was about.

"Looking into your daughter's death," I said.

It wasn't exactly a lie.

He remained silent for another moment. "I'll be right there."

Miles opened the door a moment later and surveyed us with suspicious eyes. Miles was an imposing figure—6'2", square jaw, ice-blue eyes, and silver hair. Though he was probably late 40s or early 50s, he had an athletic physique and looked like he pumped a lot of iron. The recent death of his daughter had given him an angry disposition. "The medical examiner ruled her death accidental. Has something changed?"

"I'm sure you're aware that Alaric Vesper is deceased," I said.

"Good riddance. Maybe there is justice after all."

"I'm aware you believe he's responsible for your daughter's death. Do you have any thoughts about a potential motive?"

"Stacy was pregnant."

That hung there for a moment.

"I think that threatened to disrupt his marriage, and I don't think he had any intention of leaving his wife. It was easier to make Stacy go away. I warned her about that scumbag. She wouldn't listen to me. I got a bad vibe the first time I met him." Miles shook his head. "It was out of character for Stacy to get involved with a married man. I didn't raise my daughter that way. But he had some kind of magical hold on her."

"Was she your only child?"

"No. I have a son, Garrett."

"Did you ever confront Alaric after the accident?"

"It wasn't an accident. It was negligence at best and murder at worst." His eyes filled with rage, and his jaw clenched tight. The anger displaced the pain, for the time being. "If he wasn't dead already, I'd have half a mind to put a bullet in him."

"On that note, where were you last night?" I asked.

His rage intensified, and his cheeks reddened more. His eyes narrowed at me. "How dare you come to my home and insinuate something like that!?"

"You just said you wanted to kill the guy."

"It's a figure of speech."

Miles glared at me for a moment. "You are not investigating Stacy's death. You're trying to find out who killed that son-of-a-bitch."

"The two are interrelated, perhaps."

His eyes narrowed, and he seethed with anger. "To answer your question, I was home last night."

"Alone?"

"Yes. My son was out last night."

"Garrett lives with you?"

"Yes."

"Where was he last night?"

"He was at work." His eyes flicked between the two of us. "I don't think I like where this is going."

"Is Garrett here right now?"

"He's sleeping. He didn't get off work until late. I think it was around 4:00 AM by the time he got home."

"Can we speak with him?"

"I don't see how answering any of your questions is going to be beneficial to my family. If you want to talk to him, come back with a warrant."

He closed the door and latched the deadbolt.

I shared a glance with JD.

"We need to figure out where the kid works and pay a visit," JD said.

I pulled out my phone as we walked back to the Porsche and searched for Garrett Buchanan's social media profile. I found his Instabook page, and it didn't take long to figure out he tended bar at *Shipwreck*.

We climbed into the Porsche, and I dialed Isabella.

"I was just about to call you," she said upon answering.

"Find out anything interesting?"

"Well, no other cellular devices pinged the tower from the Trask mansion the evening of Alaric's death. Just Alaric's phone. Whoever pushed him over the railing was smart enough to leave their device at home or turn it off."

"See what you can find out about Garrett Trask. I need to find out if he was working last night."

"I don't think cellular data is going to be of much use in this case, but I'll look into it."

I didn't have Garrett's cell number handy, but Isabella could figure it out with ease.

JD cranked up the engine, and we headed across the island to the warehouse district. It was time for band practice.

We zipped across town and pulled into the lot. JD found a place to park, giving himself enough room to avoid door dings from the beaters that occupied the parking lot. Some of the cars hadn't moved in months.

The usual band of miscreants loitered around the entrance, smoking cigarettes, drinking beer, and killing time. They seemed to have endless amounts of it. There were lots of jet-black hair, black fingernails, concert T-shirts, and skinny jeans. There were high-fives all around as we stepped past them into the main hallway. The rumble of a band filtered through the walls as we walked to the practice studio. The place always smelled like beer and weed.

We stepped into the rehearsal space.

Dizzy, Crash, and Styxx fiddled with their instruments, tuning up and making noise.

"Any word on my guitar?" Dizzy asked.

His custom guitar had been stolen from the parking lot of a smoke shop. It was a sweet ax, but I suspected it was long gone. We had searched all the pawn shops, looked online, checked with all the music stores, but nothing turned up.

I gave a grim shake of my head.

Dizzy frowned with disappointment. "Aw, man. I'm telling you, priority number one."

As nice as the guitar was, it was far from priority number one. But I could understand his frustration.

"I'll keep looking," I promised.

The band ran through their setlist in preparation for the Halloween bash. JD took the microphone and howled scorching vocals. As usual, the band was tight and polished, and it didn't take long for the room to fill with groupies looking for a free show.

There were perks to being the manager of an up-and-coming rock band.

13

Afterward, JD treated the guys to dinner, then we hit *Volcanic* for a few cocktails. It didn't take long for the guys to draw an entourage. One drink led to many, and we ended up back on the boat for an after-party. The moon and stars flickered overhead, presiding over the debauchery below. Beautiful women peeled out of skimpy clothing and slipped into the Jacuzzi on the sky deck.

A good time was had by all.

My phone buzzed in the morning with a call from Sheriff Daniels. I was hoping he was just calling to give me information on the Vesper case. But it wasn't going to be that kind of day.

My throat was dry and scratchy, and there is a possibility I might have been a little hung over, though I can neither confirm nor deny. "What is it?"

"I need you two numbskulls to get over to the Ravenwood Bookstore."

"What happened?"

"Just grab that nitwit partner of yours and get over here. The madness is happening again."

"Madness?"

The sheriff had ended the call.

I yawned and stretched and wiped the sleep from my eyes. It required some determination, but I pulled myself out of bed, took a quick shower, dressed, and plummeted down to the main deck and banged on the hatch to JD's stateroom.

He grunted and groaned, and I figured I would have to harass him a few more times to get him up and moving. I stumbled into the kitchen, grabbed a few breakfast tacos, and nuked them.

Not another soul stirred aboard. It was way too early after the late night we'd had.

The boat was a mess, as usual. Beer bottles and empty plastic cups littered tables and counters. I found a pair of black lace panties on the deck in the salon. It was probably time to call the maid to disinfect the boat. We had found a delightful young woman who just loved to clean, and she looked good doing it. The price was reasonable for what you got.

Coffee percolated, sending a delightful aroma through the ship.

JD staggered out of his stateroom just in time to pour a cup. His long blond hair was tousled, and his eyes were puffy and red. He still had marks on his face from the imprint of the pillow. He wanted to know what the hell was going on, but I didn't know any more than he did.

We stuffed our faces with breakfast tacos, and JD pulled himself together. We hustled to the parking lot and hopped into the Porsche. Jack cranked up the engine, and we sped across the island.

Ravenwood Books was an occult bookstore a few blocks off Oyster Avenue. It had served the needs of mystics for as long as I could remember. I'm sure they saw an influx of business around Halloween. They had a wide selection of old, first-run books, bound in leather with gold trim. Of course, you could get modern books as well, but Ravenwood's specialty was hard to find, out-of-print tomes and rare collector's pieces. You could also get more than just books. Occult-related trinkets, herbs, spices, medicinal roots, knives and daggers, canes and wands, and various charms. It was novelty for some, looking for accessories to dress up a Halloween costume. For others, it was religion, and they were devout.

I could only imagine what awaited us inside.

Lights atop patrol cars flashed, and emergency lighting from an ambulance flickered. Brenda's van was parked behind the patrol cars. A crowd of curious onlookers gathered on the sidewalk.

Jack found a place to park, and we hopped out and hustled to the scene.

Camera flashes flooded the bookstore as Dietrich snapped photos.

It smelled like incense and patchouli. There were shelves upon shelves of leather-bound books. Centuries upon centuries of esoteric knowledge scrawled on old parchment, bound by hand. Grand piles of worn books stacked upon tables—an endless labyrinth of the enigmatic. Pages scrawled and scribbled with runes and symbols, rituals lost in time. There were display cases with all sorts of knick-knacks. Behind the counter were jars of spices and oddities. Glass bottles and crystal vials full of herbs and vibrant liquids—colors that ranged from neon green to obsidian black. The tangy scent lingered, lacing the air with whispers of ancient spells. There were gemstones with vivid hues of purple and green and everything in between. Packages of tarot cards and tools of divination.

A black cat prowled the store amid the chaos.

First responders buzzed about.

Brenda hovered over the remains, examining the body on the floor behind the counter. The striking woman looked to be in her early 30s with fiery red hair that shimmered in waves to her shoulders. Her emerald eyes and flawless skin were hypnotizing, even in death. A light dusting of freckles speckled her pale skin.

An ornate dagger impaled her chest.

It was the obvious cause of death. Crimson blood had trickled from the wound and stained her dress. The blood was dried and crusted now. She'd been on the floor for some time.

EMTs and paramedics milled around with nothing to do. There was no resuscitating this woman.

A young blonde stood nearby, looking on with weepy eyes. She had short hair and elegant bone structure. Her sky-blue eyes were rimmed with dark liner, and there were traces of pink on the tips of her platinum hair.

"Cassandra Ravenwood," Daniels said, looking on with angry eyes.

He tried to maintain a degree of professional detachment, but it was tough. We all loved this town, and it was hard to see these kinds of tragedies. It wasn't always like this, but the influx of new residents and tourists, and the ever-expanding developments, brought in opportunists. You took the good with the bad around here, but it never made seeing this kind of thing any easier.

"Anything missing?" I asked.

"The register is full of cash."

"There is one thing missing," the short-haired blonde said.

14

"And you are?" I asked.

"Fiona Sable," the gorgeous blonde woman replied. "I work here. I came in this morning to open up and found her like this. The door was unlocked, and I thought maybe she had gotten here before I did, but she didn't usually get here early. Cassandra said she was staying late at the store last night. I usually open in the mornings, and she closes."

"Do we have a time of death?" I asked Brenda.

"Judging by the body temperature, I'd say between 9:00 and 11:00 PM last night."

I turned my attention back to Fiona. "Were you working yesterday?"

She nodded. "I left about 4:00 PM."

"Did Cassandra mention why she was staying late?"

"She said she had some things she wanted to sort. We got in some new books, and she was trying to figure out where to place them."

"What's missing?"

"The grimoire."

I lifted a curious eyebrow.

"A spell book?"

She hesitated, and concern tensed her face. "The Obsidian Codex."

"That's the only thing missing?"

"As far as I can tell."

"Is that book worth killing for?"

Fiona gave a grim nod.

I gave her a curious look. "Tell me about the book."

She hesitated again. "Honestly, I don't even really like to talk about it."

JD and I tried to stifle our skepticism.

"Well, it's apparently not here now," I said. "So, I don't think it can hurt anybody."

Fiona didn't seem to agree. Fear bathed her eyes. "Do not underestimate the power of the grimoire. That would be a grave mistake."

"I see."

Daniels rolled his eyes and shook his head. He muttered, "Not this shit again."

Fiona's eyes flicked at him, astonished by his remark.

"Sorry. Continue."

"Cassandra kept the book in a hidden compartment on the bookshelf," she said, pointing. Fiona escorted us around the body and opened a compartment hidden in the spines of leather-bound books. You'd never know there was a space behind those fake spines.

The compartment was empty.

"That's where she kept it?" I asked.

Fiona nodded.

"Who else knew about the book?"

"Just Cassandra and me, but..." Fiona hesitated. "That's a bit of a complex question."

"What do you mean?"

"It's not an ordinary book. And these aren't ordinary spells. It contains incredibly powerful dark magic. It's ancient. Written in the twilight of antiquity when the world was young, and the knowledge of magic was still attainable."

We all regarded her with skepticism but listened intently.

"A dark sorcerer wrote the grimoire in blood," Fiona said. "It contained his most powerful spells, derived directly from the Prince of Darkness himself."

She said it in an ominous tone, and her words hung in the air like haze.

She continued, "The book contains the power of life and death, eternal youth, and untold riches. It's highly sought after in the occult world. You have to understand, the book yearns to be found by those who would fully utilize its power. It calls out to the malevolent, and they are drawn to the book."

This was getting a little out there for me, but I kept listening.

"The Codex is alive. Sentient. It lives and breathes, whispering secrets of the arcane. It has its own desires. But the Codex comes with a curse. Few who possess the book can relinquish it of their own free will. Its allure is powerful. But what it giveth, it taketh away. The book siphons power from its possessor until there is nothing left. By the time the owner realizes their dire situation, it's too late. The effects are masked by the power of the book until they can't be hidden any longer." Fiona grew more and more dramatic with each passing phrase. "It is merciless and evil. A thing to be feared."

"Okay," JD sang, doubtful.

Fiona's eyes narrowed at him. "It would be unwise to mock the Codex."

JD's face scrunched dismissively.

"The Codex is wicked," Fiona warned, her eyes round, her tone ominous. "It devours souls."

"If it was so dangerous, why did Cassandra keep it in the bookstore?"

"As I told you, once it came into a person's possession, they were powerless to discard it. I tried to get her to part with it, but she wouldn't have it. I watched her grow more and more dependent upon it. Sometimes, I'd catch her staring at it, flipping through the pages, caressing it like a lover."

I looked at Cassandra, her beauty almost angelic, even in death. "You said the book was drawn to malevolent forces. Yet Cassandra doesn't strike me as evil."

"That's what's so insidious about it. The book takes pride in corrupting the innocent."

Sheriff Daniels was at his nonsense maximum. I didn't know how much more of this he could take.

"You think that the Codex called out to malevolent individuals, beckoning them to come to the Ravenwood bookstore," I said.

Fiona nodded.

"So, somebody came in last night and stabbed her and took the book from her hiding spot?"

"It would appear that way."

"I noticed several daggers in the display case," I said, motioning to them. "What can you tell me about the one in Cassandra's chest?"

"That was hers. She kept it on her. She used it for spellcraft and self-defense."

"So she was stabbed with her own dagger?"

"It's just the type of thing that would give the Codex joy. The irony of it. The book can turn on you like a dime."

"Did it make you uncomfortable working in the store, knowing the grimoire was here?"

"Absolutely. But what was I going to do? Quit? I like my job, and I wasn't going to turn my back on Cassandra. She needed my help. I considered her a friend."

"Let's go ahead and get this out of the way," I said. "Where were you last night?"

She tucked her chin, offended. Her brow crinkled. "You can't be serious?"

"It's a matter of procedure."

"I was at home. I took a nice bubble bath, had a glass of wine, and watched TV."

"Can anyone verify that?"

"Sadly, no. I'm single at the moment."

"I find that hard to believe."

She didn't know whether to take it as a compliment or get annoyed. "Are you saying you don't believe me?"

"I'm just saying it seems like you have plenty of opportunities for company."

The sheriff rolled his eyes.

"Can you think of anyone specifically who wanted the grimoire?"

15

"That witch across the street," Fiona said, pointing to the other bookstore. "Sybil. I'm sure she'd love to get her hands on the grimoire. She can see right into the shop. She'd know when Cassandra was alone. I'm sure she saw her fondling the book. It would be impossible for a woman like Sybil not to feel the presence and energy of the Codex."

I got the impression that Fiona was being literal when she called Sybil a witch.

"I wouldn't be surprised if she did this," Fiona continued. "The store was vandalized not long ago, and I'm sure she put a hex on us."

"A hex?" I asked, trying to hide my skepticism.

"Yes, there were various sigils scrawled in blood on the glass. It had to be her."

"Did she ever make any direct threats?"

"There's been bad blood between Cassandra and Sybil forever. I mean, she opened that bookstore directly across the street. Why would she do that? Ravenwood Books has been here forever. I'm sure there's plenty of room on this island for two occult bookstores, but not across the street from each other."

"Makes it convenient for customers," I said. "If they don't find what they're looking for in one place, they can always walk across the street to the other."

"I suppose. But still, I think she was over there, doing whatever she could do to cause our downfall. I could feel it. Cassandra could too. But she was able to fight it off."

"She wasn't able to fight this off," JD murmured.

Fiona frowned.

"Is there anybody else you can think of?" I asked.

"Aside and apart from every evil person on the planet, a few come to mind. Caspian Blackstone, for one."

"Tell me about him."

Fiona rolled her eyes and groaned. "He likes to think of himself as a powerful warlock. But the guy couldn't conjure a spell to save his soul. He came in here a few weeks ago inquiring about the grimoire. Said it belonged to his great-great-grandfather and was stolen. Said it belonged in the family, and he was its rightful heir and protector. Cassandra denied that she possessed the book, but he didn't buy it. He said it had spoken to him. He knew it was here."

"You think he's capable of murder?"

"Ordinary people will do extraordinary things to possess the Codex. The grimoire will lend strength to those that seek it if it desires a new owner." Fiona paused. "Your assessment of Cassandra was right. I don't think she was evil enough for the book. She couldn't satiate its desire for malevolence."

"Was Caspian violent? Did he make any threats when he came into the store?"

"Veiled threats. He warned that he would take the Codex by force if necessary."

I exchanged a look with JD and the sheriff.

Daniels suffered through this.

The black cat purred as it nuzzled my shin.

"I think you've got a new friend," JD muttered.

"Who else wanted the grimoire?" I asked.

Fiona thought about it. "A collector came into the shop a few weeks ago offering to purchase the Codex. Again, Cassandra denied she had it. But I'm telling you, these people knew. It called to them." There was no doubt in her mind about the power of the Codex.

The rest of us were full of doubt.

"Do you recall the collector's name?" I asked.

"Nice gentleman. Older. Quincy," Fiona thought about it for a moment. "Quincy Holloway. Didn't strike me as the type who would know about the grimoire." She paused. "Oh, and there were some kids in here last week."

"Kids?"

"Little hoodlums. 15, 16 years old. Satanic metal T-shirts. They came in, acting tough, demanding the Codex. Acted like they were some badass gang." Fiona rolled her eyes. "Cassandra turned them away, but they did threaten to come back and take it. It was a little creepy, I have to admit. I mean, they were kids, but they had auras of evil."

"Had they been in the shop before?"

"A few times. They'd look around, flip through books, but never bought anything. I don't think they had two nickels to rub together, if you want the truth."

"Does Cassandra have any next of kin?"

"She's got a sister. They're not close."

"What's her name?

"Gwen."

"You know where we can find her?"

"You're the detective. I'm sure you can figure it out."

I handed Fiona a card, and she gave me her contact information. I told her to get in touch if she could think of anything helpful.

Brenda and her crew bagged the remains and transferred the body to a gurney. They rolled the corpse out of the bookstore, and Fiona's eyes misted again as the remains passed by.

"Remind me to take a vacation next Halloween," the sheriff muttered. "You two can deal with this bullshit."

"It wouldn't be Halloween if weird stuff didn't happen around here," JD said.

"What about the cat?" I asked.

Fiona scooped the furball from the floor and cradled it in her arms. She baby talked, "I guess you're coming home with me, aren't you, Elvira?"

Jack muttered, "I bet that cat saw everything."

"Too bad she can't talk," I said.

"How do you know she can't?" Fiona quipped.

Daniels shook his head and stormed out. He'd had enough.

We followed him onto the sidewalk.

Paris Delaney and her news crew accosted us. "Deputy Wild, can you confirm that Cassandra Ravenwood is, in fact, the deceased?"

We had a leak in the department, and Paris had a way of acquiring privileged information almost before it happened. I don't know who she was paying or how much, but she was damn near clairvoyant herself.

"I'm sorry, but the name of the deceased is being withheld pending the notification of next of kin." I glared at her, annoyed by her presumptive outburst on live television.

While we were in the area, we decided to speak with Sybil at the *Arcana & Alchemy* bookstore.

JD and I hustled across the street, avoiding the traffic, and stepped into the mystical repository. It was similar to the Ravenwood, just not as big. It had plenty of leather-bound tomes, magical accessories, incense, and apothecary items. It was even complete with its own resident black cat. It seemed mandatory for this kind of store.

The door chimed as we entered.

"Can I help you?" a stunning brunette asked from behind the counter. She had sultry eyes that beckoned behind black glasses. Her wavy raven hair dangled well past her shoulders, and her black corset pushed together a delightful valley of cleavage that made everything else in the world seem unimportant. She had a beauty mark above her full lips. If she was a witch, she could cast a spell on me anytime.

I flashed my badge and made introductions. "There's been an incident across the street. I'm wondering if you saw anything unusual? How late were you here last night?"

"I couldn't help but see the emergency vehicles. I hope everything's okay."

"Not really."

"What happened?"

I told her.

Sybil gasped and clutched her heart. "Oh no! That's tragic." She attempted to sound sincere, but her tone seemed lacking. "Do you know who's responsible?"

"That's what we're trying to find out."

"That's frightening. It's just across the street."

"What time did you close the store last night?"

"We typically close at 9:00 PM, but sometimes I'm here as late as 10:00 PM."

"What about last night?"

"Last night, I think I left around 9:30 PM."

"You think?"

"I can't exactly be sure. I don't want to lie," she said, pressing her hand against her heart again, squishing her breasts.

She struck me as the type that didn't have any problem lying.

"Did you notice anything odd at that time?" I asked.

16

"The lights were still on in Ravenwood when I closed, as I recall, but..." Sybil's brow knitted as she thought about it, and her mouth scrunched. "Don't quote me on this, but I think I saw Cassandra through the glass alive and well at that time."

"And you didn't see anyone suspicious in the area?" I asked.

Sybil shook her head, and her raven hair swayed.

"Was there anybody in the store with her when you left?"

"Again, don't quote me on this, but not that I recall. I was in a hurry to get home. It had been a long day, I was tired, and I had plans."

"What were your plans?"

"I was meeting a girlfriend of mine at Spellbound for drinks."

"How long were you at Spellbound?"

"I think we were there until midnight, then we went to Cathedral to dance."

"I'll need your friend's name and contact information."

Her eyes narrowed with a mix of confusion and concern. "Am I some type of suspect?" she asked innocently, like it was the most absurd thing in the world.

"Just routine. Did you get along with Cassandra?"

"She was my main competition. I can't say that she was my favorite person in the world. But I had no real animosity toward her."

"That's not exactly what I heard."

"What did you hear?"

"I heard their storefront was vandalized. A curse scrawled in blood."

Sybil lifted an astonished brow. "And you think I did that?"

"I don't have an opinion on the matter. I'm just trying to collect the facts."

"I most certainly did not put a curse on Cassandra or her bookstore."

"You didn't hex your main rival?"

"I'm a believer that you get back threefold what you put out. I'm not into dark magic."

"Speaking of dark magic, are you aware of the Obsidian Codex?"

She stiffened. "I suppose you're talking about the real grimoire, not the book of the same name written by Damian LaCroix?"

"The real thing."

She shivered. "What do you want to know?"

"Were you aware that Cassandra was in possession of the grimoire?"

Sybil hesitated. "I sensed an evil presence. I suspected."

I looked through the window across the street at Ravenwood. There was a clear line of sight into the shop. There was no doubt in my mind that Sybil could have seen Cassandra with the grimoire and may have known about its secret hiding place. In a skeptical voice, I said, "You never saw Cassandra handle the grimoire?"

"I didn't make a habit of spying on my neighbor. I take it she was murdered, and the book was stolen?"

"Something like that."

"I can assure you, I didn't take the grimoire. It's deadly and brings nothing but sorrow and misery to its possessors."

"From what I understand, it's rare for one to be able to escape the book's allure."

"I don't need that kind of drama in my life."

I strolled around the bookstore and surveyed several daggers in a glass case. They were ornate instruments with intricate carvings. Similar, but not identical, to the one that had penetrated Cassandra's chest.

"Was she stabbed?" Sybil asked.

"I can't discuss the specifics of the case."

"So she was stabbed," Sybil said with confidence.

"You know a man named Caspian Blackstone?"

She rolled her eyes. "Yes. Of course. This is a small community. I think everyone knows everyone."

"When was the last time you saw him at Ravenwood?"

"I don't recall. As I mentioned, I don't make a habit of spying on my neighbor."

"Fiona mentioned having a problem with some hoodlums," I said. "Have you run into any issues here?"

She rolled her eyes. "Wanna-be gangsters. Though they kinda scare me. They're in here occasionally. They never have any money. It wouldn't surprise me if they sacrificed a goat or small child. Perhaps a young virgin." She was half joking. "Though you won't find many on this island."

"You know who these kids are?"

"I never caught their names. But if they come back in, I'll see what I can find out."

"What about this book by LaCroix?"

Sybil shrugged. "Just an homage. Something for the curious. The book puts forth theories on the origin of the Codex and speculates on the spells contained within."

I dug into my pocket and gave her a card. "Let me know if you can think of anything else."

She smiled. "I will."

She gave me her phone number and the number of her friend, Willow.

"Stop by anytime, gentlemen," Sybil said in a flirty tone as we stepped outside.

JD and I hustled back to the Porsche, hopped in, and returned to the station to fill out after-action reports. I called Willow but got her voicemail. "This is Deputy Wild with Coconut County. I need your assistance to verify a few details."

I left my contact information, then ended the call and dialed Isabella. "I've got more cell phones for you to track."

17

"**F**iona's phone was off the grid from 9:15 PM onward," Isabella said. "It popped back up around 8:15 AM this morning."

"Interesting."

"This case sounds crazy."

"It is."

"Keep me posted. I gotta hear how this one turns out."

I chuckled. "Will do."

"Oh, and FYI, because I know you're going to ask, there were no other phones within the Ravenwood Bookstore at the time of the murder. Just Cassandra's."

"Good to know."

I thanked her and ended the call.

The forensic team took the dagger and logged it into evidence. The lab would try to pull prints and other trace DNA.

"We find that grimoire, we find the killer," JD said. "Might be time to talk to Teagan's psychic friend."

I gave him a doubtful glance.

"Hey, at this point, what have we got to lose? It can't get any crazier."

I cringed when he said that. Things could always get crazier.

"And I'm not entirely convinced that the little temptress didn't have any involvement," he added.

"Which temptress?"

"Sybil. She had the perfect vantage point. She knew when Cassandra was coming and going. She knew when Cassandra would be alone. How hard would it be to walk across the street, stab your rival, and take her prized possession?"

We left the station and headed across the island to find Prim Sterling. She worked out of her house a few blocks off Oyster Avenue. It was a quaint little bungalow with yellow siding, white trim, and a forest-green door. An antique-style sign in the front yard read: *Psychic Readings, Tarot, Fortune-telling.*

JD parked at the curb, and we pushed through the gate and strolled the walkway to the veranda. I knocked on the door and waited. I figured a 90-year-old woman wouldn't be too spry on her feet, but footsteps shuffled toward the door faster than I anticipated.

Prim pulled open the door, and a look of confusion twisted her face when she saw us. Confusion turned to annoyance. "What the hell do you want?"

"You're the psychic, you tell me," I snarked.

That was probably the wrong thing to say.

Prim wasn't 90 years old. She was early 20s with golden blonde hair. She was the girl we had seen at Waffle Wizard. The one we'd stolen the parking space from.

"I'd like to apologize for my friend's rudeness earlier," I said, trying to diffuse the tension.

"What are you, some kind of stalker? You tracked me down?"

I flashed my badge.

Prim looked unimpressed. "I don't assist with police investigations."

I lifted a surprised brow. "How do you know that's why we're here?"

"I'm the psychic, remember?" she snarked back.

"Don't think of it as assisting. Think of it as offering advice. We don't normally deal with this type of thing."

Her beautiful blue eyes narrowed. "What type of thing?"

"Aren't you going to invite us in?"

"No."

"We're happy to pay you for your time," JD added.

She considered it for a moment, then stepped aside and motioned us in. We entered the house, and she led us into the living room. There was a table—no crystal ball—a few chairs and a couch. Soothing mood music, and the smell of incense, filled the air.

It wasn't as hokey as some of the fortune tellers on the strip. The ones that were in it for a quick buck and couldn't tell you any more about the future than anyone else. Though they were certainly prone to making up stuff.

Prim offered us a seat at the table and sat across from us.

"You're not at all what I expected," I said.

"What did you expect?"

"Teagan had a little fun with us."

"You know Teagan?"

I nodded.

"She's a sweetheart."

"I know."

Prim stared deep into my eyes for a moment. I didn't mind. She had eyes that were easy to look at. I could be inclined to stare at them all day.

She finally said, "I guess if you're close with Teagan, you can't be half bad."

I smiled.

"So, what brings you here? What advice do you need?"

I wanted to make another snarky response, but I thought better of it. *Shouldn't she already know?*

"There have been two murders recently," I said.

"Alaric Vesper and Cassandra Ravenwood."

I nodded.

"I'm aware. I watch the news."

"Those two run in your circles. Did you know either of them?"

"Why do you automatically assume we run in the same circles?"

I shrugged. "Paranormal activity and the occult seem to go hand-in-hand with other supernatural phenomena. You're a medium, are you not?"

"I don't like to classify myself in such narrow terms. I have certain gifts. My goal is to use those gifts for the betterment of others."

"For a price," I added.

"Takes money to pay rent." She paused. "But to answer your question, yes, I knew Alaric and Cassandra. Not well. But I knew of them. I have been in Ravenwood before."

"What did you think of Alaric?"

"I thought he was a guy that knew how to market himself. He gave people exactly what they wanted."

"You thought he was a fraud?"

"I didn't say that. Like all cops, you're putting words in my mouth. It's not my place to make judgments about other people's gifts. I wouldn't pay for his services, and certainly not for the money he charged." She took a breath. "I believe we all have certain abilities. Most people don't recognize even a fraction of their true potential."

There was some truth to her statement. "You think we all have psychic abilities?"

"I think everyone is unique. Everyone has a special gift. It's not for me to say what that is. I think it's important to allow ourselves to discover our potential."

"How does one discover one's potential?" JD asked.

"It starts with getting centered, self-reflection, awareness, listening to The Universe."

"You know anyone who may have wanted to kill Alaric Vesper?" I asked.

"I didn't know him well enough to know who his enemies were. But it wouldn't surprise me if he had more than a few."

"Why do you say that?"

She shrugged. "Call it intuition."

"Does your intuition tell you anything about his killer?"

"I told you, I don't assist in police investigations. If you're asking for advice, I'll give you advice, but I'm not going to speculate about who killed who."

"Why not?"

Her eyes flared with annoyance. "I need not explain myself."

"Fair enough. What can you tell me about the Obsidian Codex?"

Her eyes rounded, and her face stiffened. Through gritted teeth, she hissed, "Do not speak those words in this house."

I raised my hands in surrender. "Sorry."

Her eyes darted between the two of us. "I think you both should leave."

"We're just getting started."

"No, we're not. I want nothing to do with that book. It can only bring misfortune." She paused for a moment, surveying us. "Why do you mention it?"

Curiosity had gotten the best of her.

"Cassandra was in possession of it."

She looked at us with a surprised brow. "*Was?*"

"It was stolen."

She cringed.

"You didn't pick up any vibes about the book?"

"I don't open myself up to that type of energy." Her jaw tightened, and she swallowed. "The book is dangerous. It must be destroyed."

"Well, that's where you come in. You can help us, or so I'm told," I said.

"I can't help you."

"If you don't want to get involved, I understand," I said, attempting to use reverse psychology.

"That kind of thing is out of my area. I counsel people on relationships, financial matters, and life choices. I don't channel dark energy. You have to realize that book is a portal —a gateway for all that is wicked."

We both gave her a doubtful glance. I just wanted to find the book so I could find the killer.

Prim's eyes surveyed us. "You two don't know what you're getting into. I'm going to give you a piece of advice. I won't even charge you for it. Start taking this seriously. Your life could depend on it."

I'm not really sure what I expected to gain from Prim. I didn't really believe in all this stuff, anyway. But I was hoping for a little more than this.

I gave her a card and told her to get in touch if there was anything she thought we should be aware of.

She could call me just for the hell of it, and I wouldn't mind.

"What do we owe you for this consultation?" I asked.

"Initial consultation is free."

"You should let me buy you dinner," I said. "A token of my appreciation."

She didn't need to be a psychic to intuit my intentions. "No, thank you, Deputy. I don't date clients."

I smiled. "Seeing as how you didn't charge for your services, and we gained nothing from you, I'm not really a client, am I?"

18

P rim's eyes narrowed at me, offended. "I wouldn't say you gained nothing."

"You refused to help us," I said casually.

"To the contrary. I helped you quite a bit. I gave you a valid warning, and I told you the book needs to be destroyed."

"Conflicting advice. You want us to find it... You want us to stay away. Which is it?"

She frowned at me. "Those are decisions you will have to make for yourself."

I pushed away from the table. "Get in touch if you decide to be helpful."

Prim glared at me. "It's not my problem if some people don't recognize help when they see it."

I thanked her for the advice—or lack thereof—and we left.

As we stepped onto the porch and walked back to the car, I said, "If you just would have given her the parking space, she might have been more helpful."

JD scowled at me. "I don't think helpful is in that girl's vocabulary."

We climbed into the Porsche and headed across the island to find Cassandra's sister, Gwen. She lived in the Coconut Cay Apartments on Lighthouse Lane. It was an uninspired complex, but not terrible. The sun-bleached pale coral siding was faded and weathered, a pale reminder of its once vibrant color. The grounds were dotted with tropical vegetation and splashes of flowers. A few scruffy coconut palms loomed over the buildings, their fronds rustling with the wind.

The complex was a series of multi-unit buildings. There was no gated parking or other security features.

JD found a place to park, and we searched the grounds for unit B104.

Denise had already done the death notification.

We banged on the door.

A soft voice called through, "Who is it?"

"Coconut County," I said.

Gwen unlatched the deadbolt and pulled open the door.

She was technically Cassandra's younger sister, but she looked older. A little more weathered. A few more fine lines. More trauma in her eyes. She was attractive with flowing red hair, hazel eyes, and creamy skin, dusted with freckles. The resemblance was apparent, but Cassandra was the more blessed of the two in the looks department.

I expressed my condolences. "I know this is a difficult time, but we just have a few questions for you."

She nodded and stepped aside. "Please, come in."

Gwen ushered us down the foyer into the living room and offered us a seat on the couch. It was a small one-bedroom apartment with a tiny kitchen, a bar counter, and a small patio enclosed by a wooden fence. The white tile in the foyer and gray carpet weren't much to speak of, but Gwen had cozied up the place with light furniture and coastal accents. Mass-market art hung on the walls—large giclées of Impressionist seascapes.

Gwen didn't strike me as the kind of girl that would have any interest in the occult or dark magic. She looked somewhat wholesome. Then again, so did Cassandra.

"Do you have any leads?"

"A few," I said. "An item was stolen from the store. We're hoping you might have some information about that."

She shrugged. "I don't know. I wasn't in regular contact with Cassandra."

"Were you two estranged?"

"We spoke here and there, but I wouldn't say we were close."

"Any particular reason?"

"You know how it is. Family can be complicated. We didn't always get along, but I tried to maintain some connection."

"What was the issue?"

"How much time do you have?" she joked.

"I've got all the time in the world." I smiled.

"Do you have any siblings, deputy?"

I nodded. My sister and I weren't currently on the best terms, either.

"Then you know how it can be. I wish we were closer."

I could relate.

"Years of little things," Gwen said. "Grievances and slights. Those can add up over time. Put two strong personalities into a room, and they often butt heads."

"I understand."

"I'm not going to lie. The fact that my parents decided to give her the bookstore and exclude me from their will created a little tension."

I was surprised she volunteered that information. It was starting to sound like a motive.

"That probably makes me a suspect, doesn't it?"

"Most people are killed by someone they know."

"There have been a number of times where Cassandra made me so mad I wanted to kill her. Now that she's gone, I feel guilty."

"Guilty for what?"

"Not doing more to strengthen our relationship. We were all each other had. I thought my parents' death would bring us closer together, but it drove us further apart."

"If you don't mind my asking, why were you cut out of the will?"

"You get straight to the point, don't you?"

I smiled. "It's my job."

Gwen sighed as she reflected. "I was a bit of a wild child. Quite impulsive. I was always butting heads with my father. He was a lot like Cassandra, or should I say, Cassandra was a lot like him. They were two peas in a pod. They got along. They understood each other. Me and my father, not so much. I was drinking and doing drugs and getting into trouble. I'm sure my father thought that I wasn't capable of managing the business with Cassandra. He knew there was tension between us, and I think he chose his favorite. It was no secret she was the golden child. She could do no wrong."

She tried to mask her resentment as much as possible, but there was no denying it—Gwen had a lot of issues with her father and Cassandra.

"Now for the really direct question," I said. "Where were you last night?"

19

G wen smiled. "I was waiting for that. I had dinner with a friend, then we went out for a few drinks. I got back to the apartment a little after 2:00 AM."

"Boyfriend?" I asked.

"No. I'm recently single. Sebastian left me for a 22-year-old," she said, the bitter taste in her mouth almost puckering her lips.

"You can't be a day over 24," I said, attempting to flatter her. She was closer to 40.

She saw right through it. "You're too kind, but if you're trying to butter me up to get information out of me, you're wasting your time. I don't have any information, and I didn't kill my sister."

"I need your friend's name and contact information," I said.

"Certainly. Her name is Daphne Willis. I'll give you her number."

I gave her a card, and she texted me Daphne's contact information.

I asked, "Do you know anything about the Obsidian Codex?"

Her face wrinkled with confusion. "No. What is that?"

"A grimoire. A highly sought-after grimoire. Also, apparently dangerous."

Gwen rolled her eyes. "Please tell me you don't believe in that nonsense?"

"I'm just pursuing leads. I take it you're a skeptic?"

"I grew up in that bookstore around the occult and mysticism my entire life. I never saw any indication of anything supernatural. I never had any paranormal experiences. I never heard voices. I never communicated with long-deceased relatives. God knows I tried desperately to speak with my grandmother after she passed when I was a child. I remember being a little girl reading book after book, searching for the answers and the meaning of life. Trying to make sense of it all, not really understanding why my grandmother had to go." She sighed again. "In hindsight, it's best that Cassandra got the bookstore. That was her thing. It was never mine." She thought about it. "I was angry with my father at first. But maybe he did me a favor. It forced me to find my own path."

"And have you?"

"Would I still be living in this dump if I had found my own path?"

I didn't say anything.

"I'm not where I want to be, but I know I'm headed in the right direction. And, as they say, it's the journey, not the destination, right?"

"The journey is all we really have," I said.

"My thoughts exactly," she said with a smile.

I paused. "So, what happens to the bookstore now?"

"I don't really know. I haven't seen Cassandra's will. I don't know who she left it to, if anybody. Frankly, I'm not sure how much estate planning she did. I know she wasn't planning on dying. Nobody ever really is, not at that age. But fate is strange. You never know what The Universe has in store."

"True."

There was another momentary pause.

"Can you think of anyone else who may have wanted to harm your sister?"

She sucked her lips and shook her head. "I'm sorry I can't be more helpful. I'm just not familiar with the ins-and-outs of my sister's life."

"When was the last time you spoke?"

"I wished her a happy birthday back in March. I may have talked to her since then, but I don't recall."

I thanked her and told her to get in touch if she recalled anything helpful.

JD and I left the apartment, plunged down the steps to the walkway, and headed back to the Porsche.

I called Daphne Willis to confirm Gwen's alibi. I put it on speaker so JD could hear.

Just as Gwen had stated, Daphne said the two had dinner at *Beach*, then went to *Blue Ruin*, and ended up at *Bumper* at the end of the night.

"Sounds like Gwen's got a solid alibi," JD said. "We need to track down the warlock," he muttered in a derisive tone.

20

Denise ran background on Caspian Blackstone and found some interesting information.

Normally, I would expect a *warlock* to live in a dank castle, but we didn't really have any castles on Coconut Key. Not yet, anyway. It wouldn't surprise me if some eccentric billionaire built one on an island.

I wouldn't exactly call it a castle, but the Trident Tower was a luxury high-rise fit for a king. We pulled into the parking lot, and JD drove under the carport to the valet. The kid hustled to JD's door. Jack stepped out of the car, slipped a wad of cash into the kid's palm, and told him to keep it up front. The valet hopped behind the wheel and obliged, happy to drive 10 feet in the GTS.

I flashed my shiny gold badge at the glass door, and the concierge buzzed us in. The cheery blonde greeted us with a smile. "What can I do for you, gentlemen?"

"We're here to see Caspian Blackstone."

"Unit 2801. Would you like me to tell him you're here?"

"No, that won't be necessary."

Suspicion filled her eyes. "Is he in some kind of trouble?" she asked, anticipating juicy gossip.

"Just routine questions."

"That's what you always say, then you end up carting someone out in handcuffs. What did he do?"

I smiled. "2801, you said?"

She frowned and teased, "You're no fun."

We walked across the lobby to the elevators. I pressed the call button, and a moment later, the door chimed and slid open. We stepped aboard and vaulted up to the 28th floor. I rang the video doorbell at Caspian's unit.

The speaker crackled a moment later, and a man's voice filtered through. "Can I help you?"

I displayed my badge to the lens. "I'm hoping you can help us."

"With what?"

"We need some information about the Obsidian Codex," I said.

Static hissed from the speaker, and the call disconnected.

I looked at JD, not sure if that was the end of our interview or the beginning.

A moment later, footsteps filtered down the foyer. The deadbolt unlatched, and the door swung open.

Caspian stood in the doorway with a cautious look in his eyes. He was an imposing fellow with long wavy blond hair that was pulled back on the sides. He was about 6'2", 220 pounds, and full of muscles. He looked more warrior than warlock.

I was expecting a pasty face, skinny dude. Then again, this was Coconut Key. Why pay the rent if you don't like the sun?

"Why are you asking about the Codex?"

"So you're aware of it?"

"I have knowledge of it, yes."

"I don't know if you've been keeping up with current events, but Cassandra Ravenwood has been murdered."

"I heard. That kind of news travels fast."

"I'm told the grimoire was stolen from the bookstore," I said.

"That I have also heard."

"You have any idea where it might be?"

His jaw tightened, and his eyes narrowed. "If I knew where the grimoire was, I certainly wouldn't tell anyone."

"It's my understanding that you inquired at Ravenwood about the book," I said.

"You've been talking to Fiona," he deduced.

"Yes, among other people. It's my understanding that you believe the book is rightfully yours."

"It was in my family for generations. It was stolen from us. I am merely trying to return it to its rightful place."

"The Codex doesn't scare you?"

He remained stone-faced. "The grimoire is powerful and dangerous. In the wrong hands, it could facilitate unimaginable evil. My family protected the book for centuries and kept it safe. It is my duty to watch over the grimoire and keep it out of the hands of evildoers."

"You're the book's protector?" I said, trying to mask my doubt.

"It is my calling. My obligation."

I looked at him flatly, growing weary of the BS. "How did you know that Cassandra possessed it?"

"I was drawn to it. It's in my DNA to track the book down."

"I thought it only called out to malevolent beings."

"That is my gift. I can hear the call, even though I am not evil."

I scoffed. "On that note, you want to tell me about some of your prior charges?"

His face tightened, and his cheeks flushed. "Those allegations were complete fabrications. I did no such thing."

"So you're saying that the sex between you and Stella Sullivan was consensual?"

"That's exactly what I'm saying."

"That's not what she's saying."

"This is clearly a plot to diminish my capacity as Guardian of the Codex."

"Guardian of the Codex? Did you give yourself that title?"

His eyes narrowed, and the muscles in his jaw flexed. "If you've done your homework, then you are aware that Stella has recanted her testimony, and the charges have been dropped."

"How much did you have to pay her?"

"In the best interests of all, we settled this out of court. That is in no way an admission of my guilt."

"Couldn't you have cast a spell?" I snarked. "Compelled her to recant? I mean, if you are the warlock you think you are, couldn't you have prevented the allegations in the first place?"

He didn't like that. "Sometimes evil ones are able to cloak their intentions. I was blindsided."

"Where were you last night between 9:00 and 11:00 PM?"

21

"I was here," Caspian said.

"All night?" I asked.

"Yes."

"Can anyone else verify that?"

He said nothing and continued to glare at me.

"So you confronted Cassandra about the grimoire. You believe it's rightfully yours. She turns up dead, and the book is missing, and you have no alibi."

"I did not kill Cassandra. Nor did I take the grimoire."

"You mind if we search your condo?"

"I do not consent to any searches of my property."

It was the smart answer.

"I can come back with a warrant," I threatened.

"Then get one."

I didn't have enough probable cause, and he knew it.

"I'm just curious about one thing. Why protect the book? Why not just destroy it if it is so evil?"

"Destroying the book is no easy task. There is only one way. And a curse was put on my family centuries ago. We cannot destroy the book, though we are immune to its charms. A blessing and a curse, you might say. So it is that my ancestors have become guardians."

"Do you know a man named Quincy Holloway?"

Caspian frowned with irritation. "Yes. I warned him to stay away from the book, but he won't listen to me. I don't think he fully understands what he's dealing with. Most people don't until it's too late."

"If you can hear the call of the grimoire, where is it now?"

He frowned again. "I don't know. It's gone dark. Whoever is in possession of it now has used its power to cloak the book." He took a deep breath. "I will have to wait until the spell diminishes, or there is some weakness in the energy field that surrounds the Codex."

JD and I tried to keep a straight face.

"Sure," JD said. "Sounds reasonable."

Caspian's face twisted. "You mock what you do not understand. You should be wary of the book. It is mean and vengeful."

"It sounds insecure," JD muttered.

"Dismiss its power at your peril." Caspian stared at him with intensity. "You have been warned."

"Okay," Jack said, looking at him like he was crazy.

"Don't leave town," I warned before we left and headed back to the elevator.

Caspian scowled at me, then closed the door.

Jack swirled his brain with his index finger. "That guy is out there."

We took the elevator down to the lobby, said goodbye to the concierge, and hopped into the Porsche after the valet pulled it around.

I called Isabella and asked her to track the GPS history of Caspian's cell phone.

Her fingers danced across the keys. A moment later, she said, "He doesn't have one registered in his name."

That was surprising, given the ubiquitous nature of cellular devices. "Perhaps he has a healthy dose of paranoia."

"From what you've told me about this case, he's not the only one suffering from delusions."

I laughed and thanked her before ending the call.

Jack drove to the Platinum Dunes, hoping to catch Quincy at home. It was an upscale community and the prime rival of Stingray Bay. The houses were similar, and objectively, one neighborhood wasn't better than the other. But they each claimed bragging rights.

We twisted through the posh neighborhood, passing exotic cars and manicured lawns. We pulled to the curb of Quincy's sprawling mansion at 1422 Dolphin Court.

JD and I hopped out and strolled the walkway past the circular drive, which was home to a classic Ferrari Dino. Quincy had good taste.

I rang the video doorbell, and Quincy's voice filtered through the speaker a moment later. I flashed my badge and made introductions. Moments later, he answered the door with a smile, looking eager to speak with us.

Quincy was in his late 50s with wavy silver hair, a distinguished salt-and-pepper beard, and narrow blue eyes. He had tan skin, and the lines around his eyes and his forehead only made him look more dignified. He wore a cream linen suit, white shirt, and slacks—upscale casual attire for a fall day in Coconut Key. The silver Rolex on his wrist didn't come cheap, and his *Mario Augustino* loafers were top dollar. His taste in fashion was equally as good as his taste in cars.

"I suppose you're here to talk about Cassandra," Quincy said.

"Perceptive. Are you clairvoyant?"

He laughed. "No. I don't believe in that nonsense."

"Then what's your interest in the grimoire?"

"I have a fascination with rare books. I have quite the collection. It's a passion of mine, along with cars."

"You tried to acquire the grimoire from Cassandra," I said.

"She informed me in no uncertain terms that she wasn't selling. I waved a lot of money in front of her face, and she still didn't bite. Unfortunately, for whatever reason, that book seems to take hold of people. They don't want to part with it."

"I've heard."

"I realize that people have ascribed all sorts of mystical powers to the book, but I find the people's reaction to it more fascinating than its supposed mystical powers. It's just words on paper. Parchment, to be exact."

"Written in blood, from what I understand," I said.

"As legend has it. It never ceases to fascinate me how the arrangement of 26 letters can accomplish so much."

He didn't strike me as the type of guy who would stab a beautiful young woman to death in order to acquire a book, but stranger things had been known to happen.

"When was the last time you saw Cassandra?"

"I stopped by the shop last week. Her answer was still 'no.'"

"How did you discover she possessed the book?"

He smiled. "I have my ways."

"Did it call to you?" I asked with a healthy dose of sarcasm.

He laughed. "No. I keep up with the community, and I have many informants that can help me track down books. But in this case, I have to admit, I went through an unusual method."

I lifted a curious brow. "I'm listening."

"Would you like to come in? I'd be happy to show you my collection."

I exchanged a look with JD. We both smiled.

"We'd love to," I said.

Quincy moved aside, and we stepped into the grand foyer. Like many of the houses in the neighborhood, it was elegant. Travertine tile on the floors, soft beige walls, and a spiral staircase up to the second floor. Dark hardwoods.

Quincy ushered us into the study, just off the foyer. It looked like a proper library—Chesterfield sofa and chairs. Rows and rows of bookshelves with leather-bound tomes. A few books were open and on display in glass cases. There was a minibar filled with whiskey, brandy, and cognac. A humidor housed cigars. A nook by the window was the perfect spot for relaxing with a good book.

"Welcome to my domain," Quincy said in a smooth, textured voice that could narrate a documentary. "This is my happy place. Feel free to look around and peruse the books. If you find one you like, feel free to borrow it. I believe the joy in collecting is to share these wondrous works with other people. What good are they if they collect dust on a shelf?"

"That's mighty generous of you."

"I've been blessed, and I feel I should share those blessings with others who share my passion."

"If you could have any book in the world, what would it be?" I asked.

Quincy didn't have to think long.

22

"Of course, the Gutenberg Bible ranks as my number one," Quincy said. "Only 49 copies have survived. It was the first mass-produced book printed with movable type. It is perhaps the most revered and sought-after book in the world. One hasn't changed hands since 1978. That said, the Obsidian Codex would have to be my second choice. Unlike the Gutenberg Bible, there is only one copy of the Codex—handwritten. A direct transcription of the knowledge passed on by..."

"I'm aware of. Two contrasting pieces at the opposite end of the spectrum."

Quincy smiled. "Yes, indeed. They would make good companions."

"And the legend surrounding the Codex doesn't concern you?"

He smiled and shook his head. "I'm a realist, Deputy Wild. I believe in the tangible. What I can see, feel, taste, touch, smell. In all my years, I have yet to experience anything that would suggest to me that there is something more than meets the eye."

"You don't believe in the afterlife?"

"I believe we have one life. This is it. Better make the most of it. The idea that you're going to have everything that you desire in the next life seems counterproductive to me. Strive to achieve your goals in this one. Putting it off is an excuse. An excuse for not grabbing what you want and taking it."

"It certainly seems like you've grabbed life."

"I have. And I plan on living it to the fullest. Until my last breath."

"Did you grab the Obsidian Codex and take it from Cassandra?"

Quincy laughed. "I don't blame you for asking. It's your job. No. I did not kill Cassandra. I don't have the grimoire. And sadly, I don't know where it is."

"Can you provide an alibi for your whereabouts last night?"

"I can. I was with my wife. We enjoyed a meal at the Five Fathoms, then returned home and watched a movie." He paused and looked at his watch. "She should be returning shortly. She went out to run a few errands."

"You never told me how you found the grimoire," I said.

"A delightful young woman named Prim Sterling."

That hung there for a moment.

"She helped you find the Obsidian Codex?"

"It took some convincing and a considerable amount of funds, but she was willing to embark on the endeavor. I didn't hear from her for months, then suddenly got a call one day. She told me where I could find the book, and I believe she was correct. I never saw it myself. Of course, Cassandra denied possessing the book. But I could see in her eyes that it had a grasp on her."

"I thought you said you didn't believe in that kind of thing."

"I said that *I* don't believe in that kind of thing. I didn't say that others didn't." He paused. "Maybe it's just me. Maybe I'm wrong. Maybe I'm just unable to see what others are able to see. Unable to hear what others are able to hear. My experience with this life is one of the practical. For some, theirs is one of the supernatural. Who's to say who's right and who's wrong? I can only live in my reality, and they can only live in theirs."

"Don't you think there is one objective reality?" I asked.

"We each see the world through different eyes. Who's to say this all isn't a figment of my imagination? Who's to say what's real?"

"As Descartes says, *I think, therefore, I am*," JD interjected.

Quincy smiled. "Indeed. But what do you really know about the external world? Only what your senses tell you. Your senses could deceive."

"I know that when I stub my toe, it hurts. That's all the proof I need to know the external world is real."

"But what if that's part of the program?"

"You think life is a computer simulation?" I asked.

He grinned again. "Who's to say?"

I don't think he really believed that, but he was more than happy to postulate theories about the nature of our existence. He liked *thought experiments*. But we were starting to go down a rabbit hole, and I tried to get us back on target. "Either way, I need to find out who killed Cassandra Ravenwood."

"I wish I could help you, but I don't have the answers you seek."

The front door opened, and Mrs. Holloway entered with upscale shopping bags dangling from her hands.

"Hello, dear. You're just in time to meet these wonderful deputies." Quincy introduced us. "Please tell these gentlemen my whereabouts last night."

Her nervous eyes flicked from Quincy to us. "Is he in some kind of trouble?"

"No trouble, ma'am. Just a routine investigation."

She confirmed what Quincy had told us.

An accomplished smile tugged Quincy's face. "You see, gentlemen? I am not your killer."

"It appears that way for now. But have no doubt, I will look further into the situation."

"I trust that you will. Dig deep enough, gentlemen, and you will find the truth."

I thanked him again for his time. We shook hands, and he escorted us out of the house.

"Think his wife is lying?" JD asked as we walked back to the Porsche.

I shrugged. "One way to find out."

I pulled out my phone and made a few calls.

23

"**Y**ou failed to mention a few key things when we spoke," I said, annoyed.

"I'm under no obligation to tell you anything," Prim replied, her voice crackling through the speaker in my phone.

"It would have been useful information."

"I told you when you first arrived, I didn't want to discuss that subject. I didn't want to mention the name of that book whatsoever. I don't see the harm in not disclosing that information. You found out anyway. You're clearly good at what you do."

"Do you know where the book is now?"

"No. And even if I could figure it out, I don't want to get involved."

"You got involved when Quincy waved a bunch of money in your face."

"I didn't realize what I was getting into at the time. You don't understand. That book is pure evil. I had nightmares for months after opening myself up to its energy. Strange things happened around here. Malevolent spirits were constantly attacking."

I rolled my eyes. "If you say so."

"I'm saying so! Choose to believe what you will."

"I believe that I need to find out who killed Cassandra Ravenwood."

"If you're smart, you'll let this one go."

"I guess I'm not smart," I snarked.

I ended the call in a huff, then dialed Isabella. "I have another favor."

"Not surprising."

"I need you to check Quincy Holloway's cell phone and tell me where he was last night."

Isabella tapped the keyboard, and a few moments later, she told me that Quincy's cell phone was at the Five Fathoms, just as he said. After that, the device returned to the Platinum Dunes mansion. "Looks like he's telling the truth."

"Maybe he gave his phone to his wife. She had dinner by herself while he was out going stab happy, looking for the grimoire."

"That's what I love about you. You never take anything at face value. But I think you're reaching on this one."

"It wouldn't be the first time something like that has happened."

"I'm sure you'll figure it out."

I ended the call, and we headed to Oyster Avenue to grab lunch at Pirate's Plunder. Jack ordered the Rum-Glazed Ribs with crispy sweet potato fries and slaw, and I indulged in the Jolly Roger Jerk Chicken, topped with pineapple salsa and spicy mayo, served on a toasted brioche bun.

Afterward, we hit the pawn shops, looking for Dizzy's guitar. We saw a lot of instruments, but not the custom Viper ax. I hated to tell him, but the instrument was probably long gone. I'd keep looking, but I wasn't optimistic.

By that time, it was nearing happy hour. We hit the usual spot at Wetsuit, grabbed a few drinks, ate more appetizers, then met the guys in the band at Red November. They'd recovered from the night before and were ready to go again.

It was sometime around 10:30 PM when I got a call from Prim. "I blame you."

"For what?"

"What's happening!"

"What's happening?"

"Can you come over?"

"I'm kind of in the middle of something," I said, playing hard to get.

The music and the crowd in the background were probably a dead giveaway that I was out at a bar.

"I know you, sort of, and I'd rather not call the department for this. But I don't want to go back into the house until I know it's safe."

"You mean safe from evil spirits?" I teased.

"The back door was ajar, and a window pane was broken out."

"Somebody broke into your house?"

"That's what I'm trying to tell you."

"I'll be there in a few. Stay outside and in public view. I'll call a patrol unit for backup."

"No. No patrol unit."

"Alright, I'll be there in a minute."

I ended the call and slipped the phone back into my pocket. I told JD about the situation and said I'd catch up with him later.

"You want me to go with you?"

"Not necessary. Have fun. I'm sure whoever broke into the house is long gone."

I left the bar and caught a rideshare to Prim's house.

She waited at the curb under a streetlamp, bathed in its pale glow. Her worried eyes darted about, keeping watch on her surroundings.

I hopped out of the car and greeted her. "Are you okay?"

"Just a little frazzled," she said. "I came home, parked in the driveway, and came in through the back. I saw there had been an intrusion and called you."

I drew my pistol and moved up the walkway to the front door. I peered in through the windows, then I had Prim unlock the front door. I gently kicked it open and swept my barrel inside, the beam of my tactical flashlight slashing the darkness.

I shouted, "Coconut County!"

The immediate area was clear.

I fumbled for a light switch and clicked on the overhead. The glow illuminated the entrance.

I told Prim to stay behind as I advanced into the foyer, cleared the parlor, then the living room. I went through the entire house.

There wasn't a soul.

I returned to the veranda and invited her in. "It's all clear."

She followed me inside, and I escorted her to the back door. Shards of glass lined the tile near the back entrance, glimmering in shafts of moonlight.

"Look around and tell me if anything is missing," I said.

"Nothing's been taken," she said with confidence.

"You haven't even looked."

"I can sense that everything is in its place."

I gave her a doubtful glance.

"But I'll take a look just to make you happy," she said.

I stifled an eye-roll and followed her into the living room.

Prim surveyed the area, then darted into the bedroom.

Nothing looked out of place. Then again, I'd only been here once.

She returned a moment later. "Everything's here. Why break in if you're not going to take anything?"

"Maybe you startled them before they had a chance."

She thought about it, then agreed.

"They had probably just broken out the back window and unlocked the door when you pulled into the driveway. Likely escaped through the yard and hopped the fence."

"I didn't see anybody." Prim exhaled, breathing a little easier now. "Thank you for coming. Sorry to interrupt your evening. I didn't know who else to call."

"Not that I minded, but you can call the department anytime. That's what they're here for."

"I'll keep that in mind," she said with hesitation.

"What's your aversion to police officers?"

"Let's just say my interactions with them haven't always been positive."

"Your criminal record is clean. How much interaction have you had?"

"You ran a background check on me?" she asked, almost offended.

"I do on most people I interact with. I like to know who I'm dealing with."

"I take it you didn't run a criminal background check on my brother?"

"No. What's his story?"

"Some other time, perhaps."

I let it go. "Fair enough."

There was a long silence as we stood in the living room, staring at each other.

"Well, once again, thank you for your time. Sorry for the interruption."

I smiled. "No trouble at all."

I made for the front door, and Prim followed. "If you need anything else, don't hesitate to call?"

"Thank you."

I pulled open the door and stopped in the frame. "You might want to stay someplace else tonight until you can secure that back door."

"Good idea."

"You have a place to go?"

"I can call a friend." She paused. "What about my stuff?"

"Do you have a gun?"

"No."

"If you stay, how do you plan on defending your home against intruders?"

She shrugged, then admitted, "I don't think I feel comfortable here."

"You want me to stay with you until you secure other accommodations?"

"That won't be necessary."

I nodded and stepped outside. My hand dug into my pocket and pulled out my phone. I fumbled for a rideshare.

"You need me to take you somewhere?" Prim asked.

"I can catch a ride. It's not a big deal."

"It's the least I can do."

I hesitated for a moment. "If you insist."

I wasn't opposed to getting a ride home from a beautiful woman.

"Let me just gather a few things and make a few phone calls."

"Certainly."

I waited on the veranda for her as she stepped back inside.

She gathered her belongings, did her best to secure the back door, and returned a few minutes later.

We walked around the side of the house to the driveway and hopped into her GR Corolla in Heavy Metal Gray. With a 6-speed manual transmission, 300 horsepower with 273-foot pounds of torque, and a sport-tuned suspension, the little hot-hatch had some getup and go.

I climbed into the passenger seat and buckled my safety belt. "Did you get everything sorted?"

"Yes, I'm staying with my friend, Petra, tonight."

Prim cranked up the engine, reversed out of the driveway, and asked, "Where am I taking you?"

24

W e zipped across town and pulled into the lot at Diver Down. I told Prim to pull around by the dock.

"You live on a boat?"

"There are plenty of guest staterooms if you need a place to stay," I offered.

She gave me a suspicious glance.

"It does get a little rowdy after hours," I cautioned.

"Rowdy?"

I told her about the party nature of the boat.

She rolled her eyes. "Sounds like a glorified frat house."

I chuckled. "It's not far off."

"Thank you, but I'll pass."

"Are you sure? I fix a mean breakfast."

Her eyes narrowed as she surveyed me.

"I'll be a perfect gentleman," I said in an innocent voice. But I'm sure she could convince me to behave otherwise.

She scoffed.

"What!?" I said, feigning offense. "You're not even my type."

She arched a sassy eyebrow at me.

"Please, don't flatter yourself," I said.

She gasped. "You're not my type either."

I smiled. "See. There's no reason for you not to stay aboard the boat."

She laughed. "I can think of plenty of reasons."

There was an awkward moment between us.

"Well, thanks for the ride," I said, admitting defeat.

"Thanks for assisting me in my time of need."

"Anytime."

I said good night and hopped out of the car. I watched her pull away and speed out of the parking lot.

It wasn't exactly early, and it wasn't exactly late. I had thought about having her drop me off at Oyster Avenue to rejoin the guys, but they'd be at the boat soon enough.

I walked down the dock, waves lapping against hulls, the moon glowing the marina. It was a nice night.

But there was a problem when I got to the boat.

Scrawled in crimson were various sigils and markings. It looked like it was scrawled in blood. Somebody didn't like us investigating the case. It reminded me of the vandalism Fiona had described, and I attributed it to the Ravenwood case. But who could say for certain? Both cases dealt with the paranormal.

I dialed Prim.

She picked up after a few rings. "Is this a last, desperate attempt to get me to come back to your boat and throw myself at you?"

"No. I have a little problem. I thought maybe you could offer some advice."

"It's the least I can do."

"Come back to the marina. I need to show you something."

"No. I'm afraid of what you'll try to show me."

"I'm not trying to show you that."

"This sounds like a ploy to me."

"It's no ploy." I described the situation.

25

"I warned you," Prim said, surveying the bloody scribble. "This is bad. Somebody has put a hex on you."

I rolled my eyes.

"I'm serious. And you need to take it seriously, too."

I shook my head. "No offense. But I just don't believe in that kind of thing. This is an act of vandalism, nothing more. It's connected to one of the cases, and if I can find out who did it, I might be a step closer to the killer."

Her eyes narrowed at me. "Then why did you call me to come back and look at it?"

"Where did these markings come from?"

"They are common symbols in the occult."

"Are they from the grimoire?"

"I don't have intimate knowledge of the Codex. Nor do I want to. My advice... Get a new boat."

I laughed. "I like this one."

"Now I'm certainly not spending the night aboard."

"So you were considering it?" I said with a hopeful voice.

She sneered at me. "You're impossible." Those enticing blue eyes stared up at me, and her voice softened. "I know you think this is crazy, but this is nothing to play around with. You need to be on the lookout for bad omens."

I stifled another eye-roll.

"Sudden illnesses, unexplained phenomena, visitations..."

"Visitations!?" I asked in a doubtful voice.

"Yes. Anything is possible. We don't know the extent of the damage or what kind of demons will be evoked by this curse."

"I'll be on the lookout," I said with more than a hint of sarcasm.

Prim huffed. "Ignore my warnings at your own peril!"

"I think I've had enough doom and gloom for one night."

"I'm just trying to help. I can see that help is not wanted, so I'm going home. Well, not home. But I'm leaving. Have a nice life. Live it how you choose." She spun around and headed toward the parking lot.

"I didn't say that your advice wasn't appreciated," I shouted.

"Yeah, yeah," she muttered as she marched away.

I caught up with her and escorted her back to the parking lot. "I really do appreciate your assistance."

"You're just trying to get into my pants."

"Who, me?" I crinkled a dismissive face. "Totally not interested. Besides, you're not wearing pants."

She gave me a look and climbed into her car.

I watched her go, then returned to the *Avventura*. I snapped a few photos of the curse and called the forensic team out to take samples of the blood. I checked the security footage from the aft deck, but there was nothing but static during the timeframe of the vandalism.

Everything else was normal.

It was odd.

I didn't attribute it to the paranormal. There had to be some kind of logical explanation. But still, it was a little weird.

I cleaned the blood from the boat after the forensic team had collected evidence. I would talk to the neighbors in the morning and see if they had witnessed anything.

I was expecting the guys to show up a little after 2:00 AM with an entourage, but JD returned alone. He staggered in with red eyes, looking like he'd had quite a few.

"Where is everybody?" I asked.

"There at a party in the Platinum Dunes."

"Why are you here?"

"I'm tired, and my stomach's a little upset." He made a pained face. "What happened with your emergency?"

I filled him in on all the details and told him about the vandalism that had occurred on the boat.

He was just as dismissive as I was. "I'm gonna hit the rack. I'll see you in the morning."

JD staggered off to his stateroom, and I took Buddy out for a quick walk. It was too bad he couldn't tell me who had vandalized the boat. I'm sure he'd seen it all and barked up a storm. Poor guy was a little rattled.

We returned to the *Avventura* and settled into my stateroom. Buddy curled up at the foot of the bed. I dozed off and had spooky dreams.

I was awoken in the middle of the night by a thump, and I didn't know if it was real or if I had dreamt it.

I pulled the covers back, slipped out of bed, and grabbed my pistol from the nightstand. Prim's warning had made me a little paranoid.

Buddy perked up and jumped off the bed. He barked at the hatch to the forward companionway. I put him into the en suite and closed the door. I wanted him out of harm's way.

He kept barking.

With caution, I pulled open the hatch to the companionway and scanned the area. "JD, is that you?"

Nothing but darkness.

I flipped on the light and advanced down the corridor, past the lounge and the movie theater, and held up at the hatch to the wheelhouse. I twisted the handle and opened the hatch. My barrel swept the compartment.

It was empty.

I backtracked and crept down the central staircase to the main deck. From the corner of my eye, I saw a shadowy figure dart across the salon.

I swung my barrel aft, advanced to the entryway of the salon, and flicked on the light.

The compartment was empty.

I stepped inside, moved to port, and took the passage toward the galley. "JD, is that you?" I hissed into the darkness again.

I flipped on the light in the galley and cleared the corners.

There was no one there.

My mind was playing tricks on me. A combination of nightmarish dreams and Prim's dire warning.

Just to be sure, I took the steps down to the crew quarters and searched the area as well as the guest staterooms and the engine room, then returned to the aft deck. I looked over the marina and scanned the dock.

There was nobody in sight.

The place was quiet.

I was reasonably certain there was no one aboard the boat. I checked the sky deck for good measure, then returned to my stateroom. I let Buddy out of the en suite. He still barked and trembled.

I knelt down and petted him. In a soothing voice, I assured, "It's okay. There is nobody here."

It took a little convincing, but he finally settled down.

I crawled back into bed and tried to get some sleep, but I never fully dozed off. I was always half awake.

It wasn't long before the morning sun beamed in through the cracks in the blinds, and I decided to pull myself out of bed.

I stumbled down to the galley and started grilling up breakfast. The smell of bacon and coffee did little to rouse JD. I figured he tied one on, so I let him sleep in.

I got a workout in, then took Buddy for a run around the island. It was almost 11:00 AM when I got back to the boat. From what I could tell, JD hadn't left his stateroom.

I banged on the hatch. "You alive in there?"

26

The groan that emanated from the stateroom told me that JD was still alive, though he didn't sound too good. I opened the hatch and looked in on him. "Get your ass up. It's almost noon."

He groaned again.

"Are you okay?"

"Yeah. I'm fine. I just feel like ass."

"You need to hydrate and get something to eat."

He muttered something.

My phone buzzed with a call from Brenda. I pulled the device from my pocket and swiped the screen.

"I've got bad news."

I cringed. "What is it?"

"The dagger used to stab Cassandra Ravenwood... It's missing."

"What do you mean, *it's missing*?"

"I thought the phrase was pretty self-explanatory."

"How does a piece of evidence go missing from the property room?"

"You tell me."

"Were we able to collect samples?"

"No, because I don't have the dagger."

I asked, "Who logged it into evidence?"

"Phil."

"Did anybody check it out?"

"Nope."

"Have you talked to the guys in the property department?"

"Yes," Brenda said. "They're looking."

"Maybe it's just misplaced."

"I hope so. Without a murder weapon, we don't really have a case."

It wasn't impossible to secure a conviction without a murder weapon, but it was a lot harder.

"You still have the body, don't you?" I snarked.

"I'm not *that* incompetent."

It was almost impossible to secure a murder conviction without a body.

"Keep me posted," I said.

"Will do," Brenda replied. "I just wanted to brighten your day."

"Thanks," I said, unenthused.

I ended the call and slipped the phone back into my pocket. I harassed JD again. "Come on. Suck it up, buttercup."

He pulled back the covers, sat up, and tried to adjust to the harsh reality of being awake.

To be honest, he looked like hell.

His hair was disheveled, his eyes red and glassy. He just looked uncomfortable. Jack climbed out of bed and staggered into the en suite, and I stepped into the galley to whip up a little breakfast for him. He finally staggered out and grabbed a cup of coffee. He sat at the breakfast nook, looking like death warmed over.

I found a bottle of cherry *PowerSports*™ and handed it to him. "Hydrate."

With the amount of alcohol he'd had the night before, I'm sure he was extremely dehydrated.

"You gonna make it? Or do I need to call the EMTs?"

He sneered at me. "I'm fine. I just need a minute to recharge."

My phone buzzed again. This time, I didn't recognize the number. I didn't particularly like to answer unknown calls and loathed telemarketers. "Hello?"

"Is this Deputy Wild?"

"It is. Who's calling?"

"They gave me your number at the department. I saw you on TV. You're investigating the murder of Alaric Vesper, right?"

"I am. How can I help you?"

"My name is Nora Gomez. I think I know why Alaric was killed."

She had my full attention. "I'm listening."

"I hired him to contact my daughter, Teresa."

"I'm assuming your daughter is deceased," I said.

"She's been missing for several weeks. I knew right away something terrible had happened. That suspicion was confirmed when Alaric made contact with her."

By this point, I was getting used to outrageous claims. I went along with it to see where it would lead. "Please continue."

"This is all my fault. I think I may have gotten him killed."

"How so?"

"Alaric told me he made contact with my daughter. He said he was getting close to learning the identity of her killer. I made a post on social media that I had hired him and that he was closing in on her murderer. I think she was killed by someone she knew, and they saw my post on social media, got nervous, and decided to kill Alaric before they got caught."

It sounded like a stretch to me, but I played along. "You have any evidence to suggest that your daughter is, in fact, deceased?"

"A mother knows these things."

I wasn't going to argue with her.

"And I think I know who did it."

"Who?

27

"I feel like her killer is someone she knew," Nora said. "Someone she went to school with. I just needed proof."

"Any information Alaric may or may not have gained from his *insight* wouldn't constitute proof in a court of law."

"I know. But it would be something to go on. All I have right now is a hunch. My gut instinct."

"What does your gut instinct tell you?"

"That little gang of hoodlums that terrorizes the neighborhood is responsible."

"Do you have any names?"

"Pablo Rodriguez. That boy has evil in his eyes. And I've seen the way he looks at my daughter." She corrected in a somber voice, "The way he *looked* at her."

"Did you ever make a police report?"

"Yes, and it didn't do any good."

"Do you remember the deputies you dealt with?"

"Driscoll and Pruitt," she said, annoyed. "Absolutely worthless. They've done nothing. They told me she probably ran off with friends and would be back in a few days. They said this kind of thing happens all the time. I tried to tell them that this was different. I could sense that something was wrong. They wouldn't listen to me." She paused, and her voice quivered. "You will listen to me, won't you? I've seen you on TV several times. You always solve these crimes. I know that you care. You're a kind man. I can see it in your eyes."

"I'll do everything I can. I promise. Just don't give up hope yet."

"For my daughter, there is no hope. I can only pray for justice. I've got nowhere else to turn. I spent all my money hiring Alaric. I had to sell my car to pay his fee."

I felt terrible about her situation. Her pain was evident.

"Tell me more about your daughter's disappearance," I said.

"It was a school night. She had been at a friend's house. I have strict rules. Teresa was supposed to be home by 10:00 PM. She said she was just going over to Anna's to study. When she didn't come home on time, I got worried. It was unlike her. She was always punctual. I never had any problems with Teresa. I called her cell phone, but she didn't answer. I sent text messages but got no reply. I called Anna. She said that Teresa had left and was on her way home."

"Where is home?"

"Jamaica Village."

"I'll need Anna's contact information. Just text it to me after we hang up."

"I will. God bless you."

I told her I would look into the case and report back.

I ended the call and dialed Denise. "What can you tell me about Teresa Gomez? She's been missing for a few weeks."

Denise tapped the keys and, a moment later said, "Reported as missing. Hasn't turned up yet. Looks like a request was put in with her cell provider for records, but they haven't complied as of yet."

"Dig into this and see what you can find out."

"I'm on it."

"While I have you, what can you tell me about Pablo Rodriguez?"

Her fingers tapped the keys again. After a moment, she gave me a list of his impressive accomplishments. "Well, let's just say he's getting off on the wrong foot—petty theft, vandalism, trespassing, possession of marijuana, minor in possession... the list goes on."

"Sounds like he's heading down the wrong path."

"He's already reached his destination," Denise said.

"Current address?"

"I'll text it to you."

I thanked her and ended the call. My phone buzzed with the info a few moments later.

"You up for running down a few leads?"

From the look on his face, JD wasn't going anywhere.

28

Pablo lived in the Seashell Sands apartments on Turtle Trail. It was a dull brown building with beige trim in the heart of Jamaica Village. JD had mustered enough strength to make the journey, but I drove. The Ferrari stuck out like a sore thumb.

I parked at the curb, and we ambled up the walkway to unit #105. I banged on the door, and a moment later, a woman's voice seeped through. "Who is it?"

"Coconut County," I said. "Need to ask you a few questions."

Noise from the TV spilled through the door. The woman pulled it open and surveyed us with concern. "Is there some kind of problem?"

Lorena Rodriguez was mid-30s with wavy brown hair, brown eyes, and a generally annoyed disposition.

"We're just in the neighborhood, speaking with residents. Have you seen this girl?" I asked, displaying a picture of Teresa Gomez on my phone.

Lorena glanced at the image for a fraction of a second. She shook her head. "No. I've never seen her before."

"Is your son at home?"

She hesitated.

"Teresa is about his age. He might know her."

Lorena shouted down the foyer. "Pablo! Two police officers are here."

He emerged from the hallway and appeared in the foyer behind her with worried eyes. He swallowed hard when he saw us. "What do they want?"

"They're looking for someone. A girl."

He froze.

Lorena glared at him. "Just come take a look at this picture so they can be about their way."

Pablo hesitated and swallowed hard. His eyes flicked from his mom to us. He knew exactly why we were here.

The kid took a cautious step down the foyer, moving toward us. Pablo had long, wavy, dark hair that hung well past his shoulders. He wore a black T-shirt with the logo of an old-school heavy metal band on it. I liked heavy metal as much as the next guy. A metal T-shirt didn't make him a criminal, but Pablo was no stranger to crime.

I showed him the picture of Teresa.

"Yeah, I know her," he said.

"You go to school with her, don't you?"

"Yeah, but I ain't seen her in a while."

"She's missing."

"That's terrible." He didn't sound sincere.

"When was the last time you saw her?"

"I don't know. Probably a few weeks ago."

"Where did you see her? At school?"

"Yeah."

"See, that's funny because you dropped out." Denise had given me his background.

"You dropped out?" his mother snapped, shocked.

"I didn't really drop out. I just been having other things to do."

"What other things?" I asked.

"You know, just stuff. Looking for a job, man."

JD scoffed.

"You mind if we take a look around the apartment?" I asked.

"Why do you want to do that? Teresa ain't here."

"You know where she is?"

"No."

At this point, I was looking for any excuse to get into the apartment. I needed reasonable suspicion to believe that a crime was in progress. I was hoping to smell the odor of marijuana. Something. Anything.

But no dice.

I figured we had spooked the kid pretty good. I didn't want him destroying evidence between now and the time I could get a warrant. Who knows when that would be? As it stood, we didn't have enough.

I backed off a little. "You know who she hung around?"

"Not really."

I lied. "Teresa's mother seems to think she was picked up by an older friend of the family. You didn't happen to see her get into a white pickup truck, did you?"

"Like I said, I ain't seen her since I dropped out."

"We're gonna have a talk about that, young man," his mother chastised.

I gave him a card. "Do me a favor. Talk to your friends, ask around. See if anybody knows anything."

"Sure thing," he said, having no intention of doing so.

He closed the door, and I heard him grumble to his mother. "I told you, never open the door for cops! They're just looking to cause trouble."

"You know anything about that girl?"

"No."

Their hushed voices faded as they drifted away from the door.

JD and I made our way back to the Ferrari. Jack was dragging ass.

"Maybe you should sit out for the rest of the day," I suggested.

His face twisted. "Nonsense. I'm fine. I just need to get my second wind."

We climbed into the car, and I cranked up the V8. The white Ferrari growled to life.

JD said, "That little shit knows exactly where Teresa is."

I agreed.

We drove to Anna's house. She only lived a few blocks away in a small one-story on Flamingo Park. A low chain-link fence surrounded the yard, which was a little overgrown. There wasn't much in the way of landscaping.

I parked at the curb, and we hopped out, strolled the walkway, and stepped onto the creaky front porch. I knocked on the door.

A moment later, a young girl, who I assumed was Anna, answered. She had shoulder-length dark hair and hazel eyes. She was skinny and had a narrow face.

I flashed my badge and made introductions. "We're looking for Teresa Gomez. We're hoping you might be able to help us?"

"I told those two deputies everything when they came by a few weeks ago." She was cautious and uneasy.

"We'd just like to go over it again with you."

"Sure," she said, somewhat nervous, her eyes flicking between the two of us. "You don't look like cops."

"We get that a lot," I said. "It's my understanding that Teresa was here the night she disappeared."

Anna nodded.

"What time did she leave?"

"9:30 PM or so," she said with a shrug. "She only lives a few blocks away. Her mom wanted her home by 10:00 PM."

"You know if she was going anywhere after she left here?"

"I think she was going home."

"What did you two do while she was here?"

"What does that matter?" she asked, growing defensive.

Something was up.

She was a little too skittish about the whole thing.

"I'm just trying to get a sense of what happened that night."

"We had a math exam the next day. We were studying."

"What was on the exam?"

"How is that going to help you find Teresa?"

"You know Pablo?"

She swallowed and nodded. "Yeah."

"Teresa's mother seems to think Pablo had some involvement. What do you think?"

She hesitated.

I took a shot in the dark. "Has Pablo threatened you?"

Anna's face tensed. She didn't need to answer the question verbally. She'd already done so with her involuntary response.

"You need to tell me the truth," I said. "Now. No more games."

She hesitated and shifted uncomfortably. "Okay," she exhaled. "Teresa was here, but she left early. She wanted to go to a party at Pablo's. I was supposed to cover for her if her mom called."

"She liked Pablo," I surmised.

"Big time. She had a major crush on him."

JD's face crinkled. "That kid? Why?"

"That's what I said," Anna replied. "I don't know. She just had a thing for him. I told her he was bad news. Pablo's mother was out of town, and he had a little party. Teresa wanted to go."

"Why didn't you go?"

"I don't like Pablo or the people he hangs out with."

"Why didn't you say anything when the deputies first spoke to you?"

"I did. I told them she left at 9:30 PM and may have stopped by a friend's house on the way home. I mentioned Pablo's name, but I didn't tell them about the party or that she left here around 7:30 PM. I didn't think it would make a difference. I guess the deputies stopped by and talked to Pablo. He was up my ass and told me to keep my mouth shut. I asked him what happened to Teresa, and he said she never showed up. He said he'd kill me if I tried to implicate him." She paused, fear filling her eyes. "You're not going to tell him I said this, are you?"

"We'll handle Pablo. We're gonna need you to come down to the station and make a sworn affidavit."

"What does that mean?"

"You're going to sign a written statement that says just what you told us."

"I don't know if I can do that. I gotta live in this neighborhood. I don't need those guys after me."

"Pablo and whoever else was involved are going to be behind bars."

"Can you guarantee that?" She was pretty smart for a 15-year-old. Street savvy.

"Is your mother around?" I was hoping maybe she could talk some sense into the kid.

"She's not here."

"You know when she's coming back?"

"I don't know."

I couldn't compel her to make a statement. "Was Teresa a good friend of yours?"

"She was my best friend."

"You want to see her killer brought to justice, don't you?"

"Yeah. Of course."

"You need to do the right thing."

She bit her bottom lip and shifted on one hip as she thought about it.

29

Anna agreed to make a statement, but Judge Echols wouldn't sign off on the warrant. By itself, Anna's statement wasn't enough, and more supporting evidence would be necessary.

I got more supporting evidence when Isabella called a few moments later. But I wouldn't be able to use it.

"I looked up the GPS history of Teresa's cell phone like you asked," she said. "The night she disappeared, she was at Anna's until 7:42 PM. From there, it looks like Teresa started walking home. But she made a detour and went to Pablo's apartment. The phone stayed there for almost 2 hours. Then it moved to Salt Point Harbor and went off the grid."

I cringed. "That doesn't sound good."

"The device never popped back up after that. So..."

I knew what it meant, and I was beginning to think Nora was right. Teresa was no longer alive.

I thanked Isabella for the information, then spoke with the sheriff. "We need to get a dive team over to Salt Point."

"What are they looking for?"

"The body of Teresa Gomez."

30

It was worse than I had anticipated.

A flurry of bubbles rose to the surface, and a diver broke through the water. He spit out his regulator and shouted, "I've got something!"

That horrible sensation of dread twisted in my stomach.

Paris and her crew were there to capture every gruesome moment.

The diver swam to the dock and lifted a black trash bag out of the water that had been duct taped. Forensic investigators helped him pull it onto the dock. The green trash bag had been weighted down and double-bagged. The investigators gently removed the silver tape and opened the bag.

Inside, the severed forearms of a young girl.

There was a fake diamond ring on one of the girl's fingers and a few bracelets around her wrists.

"Looks like someone took a hacksaw to the corpse," an investigator said.

The remains had been there for weeks, and they weren't pretty. The smell soured my face. The skin had started to slough and decompose. It was pale and waterlogged. Fingerprints would be difficult at this point, but I suspected the rest of the remains were out there.

It didn't take long for the dive team to pull up several more bags that included legs, her pelvis, her torso, and her head.

This was a Halloween trick I could have done without seeing.

One look at the girl's face, and I knew it was Teresa. The water damage hadn't done her appearance any favors, but she was still recognizable.

My blood boiled.

"You know who did this?" the sheriff asked.

"I've got a pretty good idea. But I can't prove it." I explained the situation to him.

Isabella had given us the cell phone data, which she had obtained through less than legal means. We couldn't use it to get a warrant. We'd have to wait until the cellular provider handed over the records. It was a frustrating position to be in, knowing that Pablo had some involvement in her death and we couldn't do a thing about it.

Yet.

With a tight face, the sheriff said, "I want you to get that little son-of-a-bitch as soon as you can."

It was almost unfathomable to me that one human being could do this to another. The fact that the crime was perpetrated by a juvenile made it all the more horrific. I say *almost* because this kind of thing occurred with shocking regularity. Violent criminals were getting younger and younger. A sense of nihilism and nothing to lose. They didn't value themselves—how could they possibly value others?

JD normally had a cast-iron stomach, and we'd seen a lot of this kind of thing. But due to his current condition, he was looking a little green. Almost as green as the remains.

We left the investigators to do their thing and made the trip to give Nora the bad news. I dreaded the drive. Even though it didn't come as a shock, it was a tough pill to swallow.

I promised her we'd bring Teresa's killer to justice. It was only a matter of time, I hoped. I cautioned her not to take matters into her own hands. She didn't strike me as the type, but people can surprise you.

Afterward, we left and returned to Diver Down to grab lunch, though we'd pretty much lost our appetites.

Teagan took one look at JD and asked, "What's the matter with you?"

"He's a little under the weather," I said.

"Too much to drink last night?"

"I think I'm coming down with something," he said, beginning to sound stuffy.

Teagan took a step back. "Stay away from me. I don't need to catch anything. I can't afford the downtime."

He frowned at her. "I'm fine."

"Want some chicken soup?"

He thought about it for a moment.

"You know, that's probably not a bad idea."

"Well, the closest thing I've got is chicken tortilla soup."

"I'll take it."

Teagan's mesmerizing eyes glanced at me. "And for you?"

"I'll take the Diver's Special." It was a platter of coconut-crusted shrimp, crispy calamari, fried plantains, and a zesty mango dipping sauce.

"Excellent choice," she said with a smile.

She placed our order, then asked about the body that was found at Salt Point. She'd seen it on the news. I gave her the details, and she was mortified by the story.

"So, what did you want to talk about?" I asked when things slowed down.

She hesitated, and a sad look filled her eyes. Her mouth scrunched as she debated her words. "I got a job offer."

"What!? Where?"

"I can't say. I'm sworn to secrecy."

I gave her a look.

"It's managing a new restaurant that's opening up. It's good money, and I'd be in charge."

"What's *good money*?"

"More than I'm making here."

"You're not really thinking about leaving, are you?"

She shrugged. "I don't want to."

"You can't leave," I said. "This place needs you. I need you."

The sheriff called, interrupting the discussion. "Denise rattled some cages and got the cellular data. Echols signed off on the warrant. Erickson, Faulkner, Robinson, and Mendoza are going to meet you at Pablo's apartment. I want that little punk behind bars ASAP!"

"You got it!"

I ended the call and told JD the good news. I said to Teagan, "We'll discuss this later."

We hustled out of Diver Down and raced across the parking lot. JD and I hopped into the white Ferrari Spider and sped to Jamaica Village.

I didn't think that Pablo was going to cause too much trouble, but we suited up in bulletproof vests and tactical gear. Mendoza and Robinson took the rear of the apartment. JD and I advanced with Erickson and Faulkner to the front door. I put a heavy fist against the door and shouted, "Coconut County! We have a warrant!"

31

E rickson and Faulkner heaved the battering ram, pummeling the door into submission. Splinters of wood scattered, and the door flung open. The team advanced with shock and awe, weapons in the firing position.

"Sheriff's Department! We have a warrant!" I shouted again as I stormed the foyer, the team flooding in behind me. It was always a shot of adrenaline—heart pounding, senses hyper-aware. Every movement, every sound, processed and evaluated in microseconds.

Panic rounded Lorena's eyes as she stood in the kitchen. She put her hands in the air.

"On the ground!" I commanded. "Now."

She hit the tile while the rest of the team cleared the living room. Mendoza and Robinson breached the rear, and Erickson and Faulkner advanced down the hallway to the bedrooms.

JD slapped the cuffs around Lorena for the time being. We moved her to the couch in the living room.

Whatever she was cooking had started to burn and smoked up the kitchen. I shut off the gas stove.

Erickson and Faulkner had returned to the living room.

"He's not here," Erickson said, holding up a kilo of white powder that I was pretty certain was cocaine. The package had been dug into, and a chunk of the material scooped out. Either Pablo had a hell of a drug habit, or he was selling bags on the street.

I asked Lorena, "Where is he?"

"I don't know."

Erickson did a field test on the substance, and it came back with a presumptive positive for cocaine. It would need to be verified by the lab, but it was enough for an arrest.

"You're in a lot of trouble," I said to Lorena.

"That's not mine."

"It's in your home, and the lease is in your name. You're responsible for the contents of this apartment. I don't know if you're aware, but that's a lot of cocaine. That's more than a personal use amount. You know what that means?"

She shook her head.

"That means possession with intent to distribute. You could be looking at up to 30 years."

Her eyes widened.

"It would be in your best interest to tell me where Pablo is."

"He left. He didn't say where he was going."

"Do you know when he's coming back?"

"The kid does what he wants. He'll be back when he's back."

Mendoza Mirandized her and escorted her out of the apartment. A crowd of curious neighbors had gathered, and the ambitious blonde reporter was on the scene. Paris had arrived just in time to capture footage of Lorena being marched out of the apartment, her wrists behind her back. Mendoza stuffed her into the back of a patrol unit.

JD and I searched the kid's bedroom.

It was a spooky, messy room with posters of metal bands on the walls, along with hot rods with flame paint jobs. Bikiniclad beauties provided inspiration for adolescent fantasies. All pretty normal stuff for a teenage boy.

It deviated from the typical décor with the addition of several satanic images. Posters of a Baphomet, an inverted pentagram, and an illustrated painting of a beautiful nude young girl on the sacrificial altar, bound about the wrists and ankles. A demonic figure with horns and a robe held a dagger high, ready to plunge it into the nubile's heart.

It was a poster for the metal band *Sacrificial Offering*. Still, in light of current circumstances, it was concerning. I began to wonder if Teresa's murder wasn't the only heinous crime the boy had committed.

We continued to search the room and found more damning evidence.

In the closet was a roll of silver duct tape, some bloodstained rope, and a hacksaw. The tool had been washed, but maybe the lab could pull trace evidence from the teeth or crevices.

I called for the forensic team, and they went through the house with a fine-tooth comb. If my suspicions were correct, Teresa had been killed in this apartment, mutilated, then dumped in the marina.

The investigators vacuumed the carpet for hair and fibers.

In the bathroom, Luminol revealed the gruesome truth.

The unmistakable glow of spatter patterns in the bathtub and on the tile indicated that the body had been carved up in this location. Investigators dismantled the drain to collect more hair and DNA.

There was no doubt that something horrific happened here. I was certain we had enough evidence to put Pablo away for a long time. Despite the fact he was a juvenile, a case this heinous would get moved out of the juvenile court system. Most likely, he'd get tried as an adult.

Daniels put a BOLO out on the kid, and Lorena was taken to the station, where she was processed and printed.

We filled out after-action reports in the conference room, then had a little chat with her. She looked frazzled under the pale fluorescent lighting of the tiny interrogation room. JD and I took a seat across the table from her.

I laid out the situation.

Terror filled her eyes, but she remained quiet.

"When the DNA comes back from the lab, it's gonna be a match for Teresa Gomez," I said. "Your son is going to go down for murder, with or without your help. A kilo of cocaine was found in your house, and you will be charged with possession and intent to distribute."

"I told you, that's not mine."

"If you cooperate and help us find Pablo, I'm sure those charges can go away."

"I'm not ratting out my son, no matter what he did."

I didn't expect her to cooperate, and I couldn't blame her.

Then she said the magic words. "I want to speak with an attorney."

That was the end of the interview. We left the interrogation room and stepped into the hallway.

Daniels greeted us with a tight face. "I want you to find that kid. I've got a patrol unit sitting on the apartment in case he comes back, but I doubt he'll show his face around there again."

"Let's look at his arrest record, see if we can figure out who his co-conspirators were, and pay them a visit," I said.

"Way ahead of you. I've got deputies looking into it."

"I'll search the kid's social media profiles and see if I can figure out who he's friends with."

"Keep me posted," Daniels said before ambling down the hallway.

Jack was fading fast. His second wind never kicked in. His energetic vigor was a distant memory. His eyes drooped, and his body slumped. His voice had grown dry and scratchy, and I'd noticed throughout the day the beginnings of a wet cough. He acted like he was wearing a weighted vest.

"Why don't you go home and sleep this off?" I suggested. "I can handle this."

Jack shook his head. "I'm not letting you chase this punk by yourself. The kid has already proven himself dangerous."

"You should take it easy."

"Nonsense. I'm fine."

Jack didn't know the meaning of *take it easy*.

I called Anna and told her we were looking for Pablo. "Do you know where he might be hiding?"

32

"He's on the loose!?" Anna exclaimed, her voice drenched in fear.

"He was not in the apartment. It's only temporary. We'll find him," I assured.

"This is exactly why I didn't want to get involved. What if he comes looking for me? What if he finds out I ratted him out?"

"We would have gotten him, with or without your help."

"Then why involve me in the first place?" she said, exasperated.

"Where would Pablo go? Who are his friends?"

Anna was silent for a long moment. "He hangs around Diego, Raul, and Carlos. It's a little gang of theirs."

I pressed her for details and full names.

"I promise we'll get him off the street."

"Did he really kill Teresa?" she asked in a meek voice.

"We've got a pretty strong case."

I thanked her for the information and ended the call.

I looked at Pablo's social media profile and was able to fill in the blanks from the details Anna had given me. His Insta-book feed was full of him and his friends partying and wreaking havoc. There were dark, spooky images of his gang practicing occult rituals.

We found Denise at her desk, and she pulled background on Pablo's band of hoodlums. They all had their run-ins with the law. Raul and Carlos had been previously arrested with Pablo, and the other deputies were looking into them. JD and I left the station to find Diego. According to the records, he lived with his mother in an apartment on Jefferson Street, only a few blocks away from Pablo's place.

I texted Isabella and asked her to locate the hoodlums' cell phones.

She messaged back a few minutes later. *[All of those phones are off the grid. Looks like they wised up and turned them off. I'll let you know if anything pops up.]*

We drove back to Jamaica Village and found a place to park. Diego's apartment complex wasn't much to speak of—multiple units of faded pastel yellow buildings with white trim. Kids played in the street, tossing a football around. We hopped out of the car and hustled through the grounds to C101. I put a fist against the door, and a moment later a woman's voice filtered through. "Who is it?"

"Coconut County. We need to have a word."

She pulled open the door with concerned eyes. "Is there some kind of problem?"

She was mid-30s with wavy dark hair that tickled her shoulders and a petite figure. She had olive skin and full lips. She didn't strike me as the type of woman that would raise a little hoodlum, but sometimes kids have minds of their own.

I flashed my badge. "Looking for Diego?"

She shook her head. "He's not here right now."

"Do you know where he is?"

She shook her head again. "Is he in some kind of trouble?"

"I'm not sure. Have you seen Pablo?"

"Not recently. Why?"

"He wouldn't be here right now, would he?"

"No. Honestly, I haven't seen him in a few days."

"He is good friends with your son, is he not?"

She nodded. "What has he done?"

"He may have killed someone," I said.

She gasped. "You don't think Diego was involved, do you?"

I shrugged.

"Diego would never do something like that. Who did Pablo kill?"

I explained the situation to her.

Sadness tugged her face. "Teresa was such a sweet girl."

"Did you know her?"

"Not well. My daughter was on the volleyball team with her last year."

"Do you mind if we look around your apartment?"

Diego's mother hesitated for a moment. "I don't have a problem with that."

She stepped aside and invited us in.

"Smells good," I said. "Lasagna?"

She nodded. "There's more than enough if you want to stay for dinner."

I smiled but declined.

It was a small, but tidy, two-story apartment with two bedrooms upstairs and one down.

We made our way through the residence but didn't find any sign of Pablo. Diego's bedroom had a similar aesthetic to Pablo's—lots of metal posters, scantily clad beauties, and satanic imagery.

After searching his place and returning downstairs to the kitchen, I spoke with his mother again and asked her about her son's fascination with the occult.

"I'm not particularly a fan of the music he listens to or the things that he puts on the walls. But what am I going to do?" She paused. "I was certainly into things that my parents didn't approve of when I was younger."

"Unfortunately, some of the fads that your son is into involve ritual murder."

Her eyes rounded. "You've got no proof of that."

"I hope for Diego's sake that he wasn't with Pablo when the murder occurred." I gave her a card and thanked her for her cooperation. "If you see Pablo, call me immediately. Just a reminder, providing him any assistance would be a felony, so I would avoid that, if I were you. Make sure Diego knows that as well."

She nodded with a grim look on her face.

She seemed like a sweet woman, but the freight train of inevitability was barreling forward, and her family was on the tracks.

We left the apartment and made our way back to the Ferrari. It had survived on the street without incident. We climbed in, and I cranked up the engine.

"I think it's time for a little hair of the dog," JD said.

"Are you sure that's such a good idea?" I asked.

"A little whiskey will settle the stomach and kill off whatever ails me."

Jack had enough alcohol in his system on a regular basis to kill just about anything, including himself.

I pulled away from the curb, and we headed up to Oyster Avenue and hit happy hour at TJ's Clam Shack. I told the hostess to seat us in Ellie's section. She was a delightful young blonde we'd met on a previous case.

"Afternoon, gentlemen," Ellie said with an inspiring smile as she sauntered to the table. "It's been a while."

"We looked for you last time we were in," I said.

Ellie frowned. "Aw, I missed you guys." Her enticing eyes focused on me. "You still owe me a night out on the town."

"I do? I mean, I do."

I offered her a protection detail when a serial killer was stalking her. It wasn't exactly an offer for a night on the town, but I wasn't going to argue with the statement.

"I've been waiting patiently. I've dropped clues, subtle hints. You're a detective. I would have thought you'd have caught on by now. How much do you need?"

"I think I got the message," I said with a smile.

"Good." She smiled back. "What can I get for you, gentlemen?"

"Whiskey. Rocks," JD said.

Ellie's sparkling blue eyes flicked to me.

"The same."

"I'll give you a minute to look over the menu, and I'll be right back."

She smiled and dashed away.

"That girl has a thing for you."

"I believe I could have a thing for her, too."

Jack covered his mouth and coughed, his lungs rattling even more than before.

"Maybe you should take it easy tonight," I suggested.

JD's face wrinkled. "I am taking it easy." He coughed again. "A little whiskey will clear this right up."

Ellie returned a moment later with our drinks, and we placed our order. JD went with the classic New England clam chowder—a rich and creamy bowl with russet potatoes, onions, celery, and spices. I went with the stone-fired pizza with gooey mozzarella, fresh basil, and tangy red sauce.

We chowed down and shot the breeze with Ellie. She made frequent stops at our table, but the restaurant was pretty packed, and her other tables kept her busy. Before we left, I promised I would take her out for a night on the town. She wouldn't have to twist my arm. It was a no-brainer.

The girl was gorgeous.

We met up with the guys at Tide Pool for our usual brand of mischief. Toned beauties frolicked in the outdoor pool, taut fabric clinging to perky peaks. There were a lot of bars and nightclubs on the island, but this was hard to beat. Chill music pumped through speakers, and the smell of strawberry and coconut filled the air.

JD bought a round of drinks and did his best to hang with the guys, but by 11:30 PM, he had to throw in the towel and admit defeat. Whatever he'd come down with was more than a hangover, and a few glasses of whiskey hadn't chased it away.

I told the guys that there would be no after-party aboard the *Avventura* tonight. There were long faces all around, but they understood.

I corralled JD and escorted him back to the Ferrari. He weaved down the sidewalk, dodging the crowd of drunk tourists. I don't think his unsteadiness was as much the alcohol as it was his illness.

We climbed into the Ferrari, and I drove back toward the marina. "You're not looking so great."

"Still better than you."

I chuckled. "You want me to take you somewhere?"

His face crinkled. "I just need a good night's sleep. That's all."

We returned to the marina, and I helped him down the dock to the *Avventura*. He made a beeline for his stateroom, and I didn't see him for the rest of the night.

I took Buddy out for a walk, then settled in and watched a little TV before crashing out. It was an unusually tame evening aboard the boat.

But morning brought trouble.

33

"I need you two numbskulls to get down to the station," Daniels barked into the phone.

"What is it now?"

"A couple of recreational divers found a sunken sailboat just north of Barracuda Key. They found a body on board. Said the name of the boat was the *Vagabond*. That vessel is registered to Jasper Armstrong."

"Where's the body now?"

"Still down there. I'm taking a dive team and the medical examiner. I'm ready to go. That's why you two need to get your asses down here, pronto."

"We're on our way."

I wiped the sleep from my eyes, pulled myself out of bed, and took a two-second shower. I got dressed, press-checked my pistol, then holstered it for an appendix carry. I hustled down to the main deck and banged on the hatch to JD's stateroom. "Get up. We gotta meet Daniels at the station."

There was no response.

I banged again, then heard a groan.

I pushed open the hatch. "You okay?"

JD responded with an unintelligible grunt.

"Divers found a body aboard a sunken sailboat."

Jack didn't seem impressed.

"Come on! We gotta roll."

"I'm going to sit this one out," he finally slurred.

"Are you alright? Do you need anything?"

"I'm good," he said in a dry, scratchy tone. "I just need to sleep this off."

I hesitated a moment. This was unusual for JD. Against my better judgment, I said, "Alright. Call me if you need anything."

He groaned again.

I'd never seen Jack like this, and I was starting to worry.

I darted into the galley, microwaved a breakfast taco, and shoved it into my mouth as I hustled out the door. I jogged the parking lot, hopped into the Ferrari, and sped to the station.

By the time I got there, Daniels had fired up the engines of his Defender class patrol boat.

I raced down the dock, cast off the lines, and boarded the boat.

"Where's the nitwit?" the sheriff asked as he idled us out of the marina.

"He's a little under the weather," I said, downplaying the situation.

Daniels just shook his head.

He brought the boat on plane as we cleared the breakwater. Mists of salt water sprayed as the aluminum patrol boat sliced through the swells. The morning sun speckled the teal ocean, and the engines howled.

I asked Brenda if the dagger ever turned up.

She shook her head. "Nope."

We skimmed across the surface, heading out toward Barracuda Key.

We arrived at our destination, north of the island, and met up with two recreational divers on a 25-foot motor yacht with a gray hull and white trim. They went over the details with us again, and the dive team submerged into the sapphire water.

It wasn't that deep here. The water was clear. From above, you could see the sunken ship below. It was a 30-foot sailboat that looked like it was in decent shape. The hull was intact, and so was the mast.

While the divers were below, I looked up Jasper's social media profile. He had once been a handsome man in his early 20s with dark hair, brooding blue eyes, and a square jaw lined with a few days of stubble. He had an athletic physique and liked to show it off on his Instabook feed.

But those days were gone. Jasper's body had been submerged for several weeks. Divers had found it in the cabin, and that had kept his body from rising to the surface with decomposition gasses. Sometimes the sea has an odd way of preserving remains, slowing decomposition. It depends on the water temperature and how exposed to the elements the remains are. Without protection, the critters of the sea will feast.

It didn't take divers long to surface with the remains of Jasper Armstrong.

He was relatively intact. The water was cooling off in the fall. But his skin was pale and breaking down, his body bloated. The man was barely recognizable. His hands and feet had degloved—a process where the skin sloughed off. It would take dental records to confirm his identity at this point. Still, I was pretty sure these remains were Jasper Armstrong. There was enough resemblance to the photos he had on the Internet that I didn't need to wait for official confirmation.

Brenda snapped on a pair of pink nitrile gloves and examined the remains once they were transferred aboard. The skin was delicate, and the slightest bit of handling caused it to tear. Just getting the body out of the water and onto the deck had damaged it considerably.

"There's not really much I can tell from here," Brenda said. "I'll know more when I get him back to the lab."

"How long do you think he's been in the water?" Daniels asked.

"Hard to say. Microbial activity will give us a clue."

I called Isabella and asked her to pull location history for Jasper's cell phone. I didn't have the number handy, but she was good at figuring out those kinds of things.

We took a statement from the divers, wrapped up at the scene, and headed back to the station.

Paris Delaney and her crew waited on the dock and gathered footage as the remains were transferred from the patrol boat onto a gurney. Her cameraman got an up close and personal shot of Jasper's remains as it was rolled toward the medical examiner's van. Brenda's crew loaded it aboard, and she closed the doors. She hopped into the van and drove away.

It was just the kind of TV that Paris liked.

"Deputy Wild, what can you tell us about the deceased?"

"Not much at this time. Boating accident. The identity is being withheld, pending the notification of next of kin."

I filled out an after-action report in the conference room, chatted with Denise for a bit, then headed back to the *Avventura* to check on JD. I had called him while on the scene, but he didn't pick up.

When I got back to the superyacht, it was just as I'd left it. There were no signs that JD had emerged from his stateroom.

I banged on the hatch and poked my head inside. "You alive in there?"

He grunted.

"You need to get up and eat something. Stay hydrated."

"I just need to sleep."

I darted into the galley, grabbed a sports drink, and returned to Jack's stateroom. I set the drink on the nightstand and took a closer look at him. "Drink some of that. It's almost noon. You had a decent amount of alcohol last night."

"Yes, mom."

"You look like shit."

Sweat misted his brow. The sheets were soaked in it.

"Have you got a fever?"

"How the hell should I know?"

"Do you feel feverish?" I asked, like he was a child.

"I'm sure I've got a little," he said. "I had chills last night. Couldn't stop shaking for a while."

"I think you need to go to the doctor."

"What for? So he can tell me I'm sick?"

"You're no spring chicken. You should get checked out. You might have pneumonia."

"Them's fighting words."

I hesitated a moment. He looked like death warmed over. "I'm gonna call somebody."

"What are they going to do?" He coughed and almost hacked up a lung.

"You could have a respiratory infection. You might need antibiotics."

"Most respiratory infections clear on their own without antibiotics," he said.

JD had an answer for everything.

"I think you need to see somebody."

"I'm fine," he said.

After a moment, he sat up, then hesitated on the edge of the bed. "See. I'm fine."

He didn't look fine.

Jack grabbed the bottle of cherry-flavored power drink, cracked open the top, and guzzled a few sips. "Happy? Can I go back to sleep now?"

"Just keep pushing fluids."

He sat there for a minute, stood up, and staggered toward the en suite. He made it a step when his knees buckled, and he smacked the deck.

I rushed to his aid. He was out cold.

34

"Jack!" I shouted. "Jack!!!"

He was unresponsive and slick with sweat. I felt his forehead—he was burning up.

I pulled my phone from my pocket and dialed emergency services.

"911, what is your emergency?"

I updated the operator on the situation, and she said paramedics were en route.

I tried to roust JD again. "Jack!"

He was still breathing, but his respiration was shallow.

I grew nervous.

His eyes finally fluttered, and he looked around in a daze. "What the hell happened?"

"You passed out."

"How did that happen?"

"You're sick."

He was all out of sorts.

I gave him a moment to regroup. "You think you can stand up?"

"Not at the moment."

Jack lay on the deck, staring at the ceiling. I think the experience threw him for a loop. Neither one of us thought he was that bad off.

The distant siren of an emergency vehicle drew close. The sound crescendoed as the ambulance pulled into the parking lot.

"Did you call the EMTs?" JD asked with an annoyed face.

"You were unresponsive."

"Tell them to go home. I'm fine."

He tried to sit up but couldn't.

"I'll be right back." I sprang to my feet and hustled out of the stateroom toward the aft deck. I opened the sliding doors to the salon and stepped to the stern. I waved to the EMTs and paramedics as they hustled down the dock with a yellow gurney in tow.

As they reached the stern of the boat, one of them asked, "What's going on?"

I updated them on the situation and ushered them through the boat to Jack's stateroom.

A fire truck had arrived along with the medical techs, and they all gathered around JD.

"Sir, can you tell me what happened?"

Jack reiterated the story while an EMT applied a blood pressure cuff to his arm and checked vitals.

"Do you have any current medical conditions?"

"Nope," Jack said.

"Any history of heart disease, hypertension?"

"Nope."

"You smoke?"

JD shook his head.

"Do you drink?"

"Occasionally," he mumbled.

I stifled a chuckle.

The EMTs picked up on it. "More than occasional. Moderate?"

"Moderate," JD assured.

The other EMT said, "His blood pressure is really low. 80/55. Heart rate 67. Oxygen saturation is low at 90." He fumbled through his kit. "I'm gonna check your blood sugar."

The EMT stuck Jack's finger and squeezed out a drop of blood onto a test strip. A moment later, he had the results. "135."

I told them that Jack hadn't been feeling well for the last day or so.

"You think you can sit up?" an EMT asked.

"I can try."

JD tried to sit up, but it wasn't going well. The EMTs helped him get off the floor and sat him on the edge of the bed.

"Are you feeling dizzy?"

"I don't feel like I want to run a marathon."

An EMT checked JD's blood pressure again, and it was still low.

The lead technician said, "I recommend you go to the ER to get an evaluation. I can't force you, but it's in your best interest. You're probably dehydrated. Your BP is dangerously low. You could pass out again. You could fall, hit your head, break something."

Jack frowned.

"Load him up," I said. "He's going."

"No. I'm not."

"Yes. You are," I said in a stern tone. There were no *if's, ands, or buts* about it. No debating. He didn't have a say in the matter.

They started him on IV fluids, transferred him to a gurney, and strapped him in. They rolled him through the boat and crossed the passerelle to the dock.

I locked up the boat and followed them to the parking lot.

An EMT asked me, "You want to ride along?"

"I'll follow."

I thanked them and hopped into the Ferrari. The EMTs closed the doors to the meat wagon, hopped in, and sped away.

It was pretty tame this time of day in the ER. A few bumps and bruises. A guy with a broken wrist. An elderly man looking frail, sucking on a cannula fed by a portable green oxygen tank. The pale fluorescents glowed, and a TV displayed 24-hour news.

JD was triaged and got a room quickly. They hooked him up with a bunch of electrodes, and his vital signs displayed on the monitor beside the bed. They drew blood for lab work and did an EKG, which came back normal.

It took about 20 minutes for Dr. Parker to look in on him. He just shook his head when he saw the two of us. "What the hell have you gotten yourselves into this time?"

I pointed at Jack.

"I'm fine," JD said. "He's just being a worrywart."

"No, he's saving your life. Tell me what's going on with you?"

JD gave him the story, and I filled in the details that Jack left out.

Dr. Parker asked Jack a series of questions and assessed his condition.

Isabella buzzed my phone, and I stepped into the hallway to take the call. "What have you got?"

"You're gonna find this interesting. Jasper Armstrong's phone paid a visit to Devon Trask before he set sail."

"What!?" I replied, stunned.

"Here's where it gets interesting," Isabella said. "Judging by the GPS data from his phone, it looks like he took a vehicle from the marina at Pirates' Cove over to Stingray Bay. He was at the Trask residence for about half an hour, then he left via the canal behind the house. The phone cruised around the island, back to the marina, then headed out to sea. It went off the grid near Barracuda Key, probably when the boat sank."

I started connecting the dots. "I wonder if Jasper Armstrong is Lily Trask's ex-boyfriend. If he was, I could understand why Devon didn't approve. Jasper was quite a bit older than Lily."

"You should have another talk with Devon Trask."

"I plan on it." I thanked her and ended the call.

Dr. Parker exited the room as I finished.

"Any idea what's going on?"

35

"He's got 103 fever and is severely dehydrated," Dr. Parker said. "We'll run some tests and see what's going on. He's probably got a bug or something. We'll see how he responds to the IV fluids. EKG was good. No sign of a heart attack."

"That's good," I replied, somewhat relieved.

"Hang tight. I'll be back to check on him."

That could have meant 20 minutes or four hours.

"You've got my number in case I have to run out for a minute."

He nodded. "I'll stay in touch."

We were in the ER so often we were regular customers. We got preferential treatment. Though that's not really the place I wanted to be a VIP.

I stepped back into the room as Dr. Parker moved on to visit with another patient.

Jack had dozed off.

I sat in the room with him. His blood pressure and O2 saturation were still borderline low.

"Don't worry," the nurse said. "He's in good hands."

"I have no doubt."

I stayed with him for an hour.

His eyes finally peeled open, and he looked at me like I was crazy. "What are you doing here?"

"Waiting to see what the hell is wrong with you."

"I'm fine. Get out of here. You don't need to stay here. They're gonna patch me up and send me on my way."

"Do you have your phone?"

"No, I don't have my phone, but there's one in the room. I'll call you when I'm getting sprung."

"I'll just hang around until then."

"In this place, that could be awhile."

I caught him up to speed on Jasper Armstrong and the fact that he visited with Devon Trask before his death.

"What are you waiting for?" JD asked. "Go talk to Mr. Trask. These cases aren't going to get solved with both of us sitting around here."

"You sure you'll be alright?"

"I'm fine. This whole thing was unnecessary. Like you said, I just need to hydrate. Now they're doing it for me," he said, lifting his arm, displaying the IV. He'd almost run through an entire bag.

He was looking a little better, but his vitals were still low.

"I'll zip over to Stingray Bay, then I'll be right back."

"I'll call you when they cut me loose. No need to come back here."

"You sure?"

"Yes. Go!"

"Hang in there," I said.

"Always."

I slipped out of the room and made my way down the seafoam green hallways toward the waiting room. Nurses scurried about, and moans and groans from patients echoed into the corridors. It was just another day of chaos in the ER.

I pushed through the double doors and stepped into the waiting area. The room had twice as many people as when we arrived. We'd gotten here at just the right time.

I stepped outside into the Florida sun and hustled to the Ferrari. I hopped in and drove over to Stingray Bay, hoping to catch up with Devon Trask. He had some explaining to do, and I didn't think he was going to be able to talk his way out of this one.

36

"I just need to ask you a few follow-up questions," I said, standing on the front porch of the Trask's Stingray Bay mansion.

Devon looked at me with eager eyes. "Certainly. Have you made any progress on the case?"

"Actually, I think we're getting somewhere," I said.

"Please, come in."

I was in the familiar position of having evidence that I couldn't use. It would take time to get the records from the cellular service provider. I figured a few direct questions might unsettle Devon.

I stepped into the foyer, and he escorted me into the living room and offered me a seat on the sofa. He called to his wife, "Vivian, Deputy Wild is here to speak with us."

"I'll be right there," she shouted from another room.

"Can I get you anything to drink?" Devon asked.

"No, thank you," I said.

Vivian hurried into the living room, and the couple took a seat on the loveseat catty-corner from me. "I'm still experiencing strange phenomena in the house. Devon thinks I'm crazy, but I think Alaric's spirit is still here with us."

"Have you hired another medium to come in?" I asked.

"No, but I'm considering it."

"I think that may be a good idea," I said. "I have someone in mind that we work with at the department from time to time."

Vivian's eyes rounded with intrigue.

Devon didn't look as enthused.

"I think that's a fantastic idea," Vivian said. "Especially since it's someone you've worked with before. Then we know they're authentic."

"There's no such thing as an authentic medium, Viv," Devon said. "It's all a hoax. I hate to say it, but Alaric was no more than a con man. He saw a couple that experienced a severe trauma, and he aimed to capitalize on it."

Vivian's jaw tensed, and she glared at him. "Alaric was not a con man. I believe that he was close to contacting Lily."

Devon raised his hands in surrender, not wanting to deal with the fight.

"There are a few things that may help us move forward in this case," I said.

"You said you had some additional questions," Devon replied. "We're happy to clarify anything that happened that night."

"Actually, I have a few questions that pertain to the time prior to Alaric's demise. Am I correct in thinking that Jasper Armstrong was the man seeing Lily?"

Devon's face tensed.

Vivian nodded.

"He was quite a bit older than she was," I said.

"That was a bone of contention, yes," Devon replied.

"She was so in love with him," Vivian said, sympathetic to the romance.

"He was too old for her, and he had no business seeing Lily," Devon said through a tight jaw. "You do know they were having a sexual relationship?"

Vivian frowned.

"I don't know if you're aware, but that's illegal in this state," Devon continued. "There were seven years between them."

"There's seven years between us!"

"I didn't meet you when you were 15," Devon said.

"You met me when I was 19," she muttered.

"When was the last time you spoke with Jasper?" I asked Devon.

"I don't know. I can't be sure."

"Has he ever been to the house?"

"Yes," Vivian said. "Several times. Lily wanted us to meet him. She was honest and explained the situation. Jasper seemed to genuinely care for Lily. You have to understand it was a difficult situation for us. Lily was wise beyond her years. An old soul. She knew what she wanted, and she was so desperately in love with him. If we would have interfered, she would have hated us."

"Parenting isn't a popularity contest," Devon said. "It's okay if your kids don't like you as long as you're acting in their best interest. Sometimes they don't know what is best for them. And Jasper was no good for Lily."

"You don't know that," Vivian snapped.

"I know that."

I interrupted their little spat. "I pulled cell records for Jasper's phone. It looks like he visited the residence on the day he disappeared."

Devon stiffened.

Vivian looked confused.

Panic crept into Devon's eyes. There was no getting out of this, and he knew it.

"He came by to see Lily," Devon said.

Devon was no dummy. He had to admit it. Otherwise, he'd lose credibility.

"Why would he do that?" Vivian asked, her brow knitted with confusion. "Lily and I were out of town then. We took a trip up to Pineapple Bay that day to go shopping. He knew we were staying there overnight."

"Maybe he forgot," Devon suggested.

"Those two talked constantly. He wouldn't just show up if she wasn't here."

Devon sighed. "He stopped by that day because he wanted to speak with me. He knew that I didn't approve of the relationship. We had a heart-to-heart talk, and I told him exactly how I felt and that I didn't want him to continue seeing my daughter."

Vivian gasped.

"I was just being honest," Devon said.

Her eyes narrowed, boiling. In a voice that could spook anybody, she asked, "What did you do?"

"I didn't *do* anything. I just made my feelings known."

"He broke up with her that night. I remember. He did it by text. Lily was devastated." Her eyes brimmed. "That's what pushed her over the edge." Vivian smacked Devon several times. "This is all your fault!"

"It's not my fault. How was I supposed to know she would react that way?"

I tried to steer things back on track. "The cellular data says that he was here for about half an hour."

"That's about right."

"Then he left?"

Devon nodded. "I never saw him after that."

"The interesting thing is he didn't leave the same way he came."

Devon shrugged. He stalled as the wheels turned behind his eyes. "That's because I gave him a ride back to his boat."

"You took him out in the canal and ferried him back to his boat?"

"Yes. It gave us a little extra time to talk. I've got a wake boat docked in the canal."

"How did the meeting between you two end?"

Devon hesitated for a moment. "I think we came to an understanding."

"Did you tell him to break up with Lily?" Vivian asked, trembling with rage and sorrow.

Devon's eyes flicked between me and his wife. A mix of fear and anger consuming him. "Yes," he blurted. "I wanted him out of her life!"

Vivian's jaw dropped, and tears streamed from her eyes. She was so traumatized she was speechless.

"How bad did you want him out of your daughter's life?" I asked.

His eyes narrowed at me, full of suspicion. "How would you feel if a grown man was banging your teenage daughter?"

Vivian gasped.

"If it was my daughter, that man might end up at the bottom of the ocean."

Devon said nothing. And, in that moment, he knew that I knew.

"You might be interested to know that's exactly where we found him," I said.

Vivian craned her neck toward me, her brow lifted. "Jasper's dead?"

"Yes, ma'am. His boat sank just off the coast. We're still investigating."

The room was silent for a moment.

"I think that's all the questions we have time for today," Devon said. "I can assure you, Jasper Armstrong was alive and well when I returned him to his boat. What happened to him after that is nothing more than fate. And if you are asking me, it sounds like he got what he deserved."

It was a bold last statement from a man that I suspected of killing Jasper Armstrong. Unfortunately, I couldn't prove it yet.

"Then you'll have no problem if we bring in another medium to try to contact the spirits that are in this house. If my suspicions are correct, there are more than two haunting this mansion."

Vivian looked mortified.

37

Needless to say, Devon wasn't receptive to the idea. I threw it out there to rattle his cage, and it did.

Devon professed to be a skeptic, but something told me he was a believer in the paranormal. I think he was afraid that Alaric might actually make contact with the departed and learn the truth. The truth that he murdered Jasper in the mansion. Devon needed to silence Alaric before he spilled the beans. That was my theory, anyway.

I called Denise when I left the mansion and asked her to pull Jasper's cell phone records through legitimate means. It would take some time, and even with those in hand, it likely wouldn't be enough to secure a warrant. There was nothing in Devon's statement that was inconsistent with the events. Just because Jasper visited his residence on the day of his disappearance didn't mean he was killed by Devon. It was suspicious, yes, but suspicious doesn't always convince a judge. Especially one as fickle as Echols.

Hell, we didn't even have a definitive cause of death yet.

I talked to the neighbors on either side, asking if they remembered seeing Jasper that day, but no one recalled anything. Nobody could say that they saw Devon and Jasper get into the wake boat. Even if I could get into the nav history of Devon's boat, it would likely only confirm his statement.

I left Stingray Bay and drove the Ferrari to Pirates' Cove. It wasn't the nicest marina on the island, but it certainly wasn't the worst. It was home to sailboats, sportfishing boats, motor yachts, center consoles, and a few houseboats. This wasn't the kind of place where you'd find gigantic superyachts with influencer models sunning themselves on the foredeck.

I talked to the manager. He told me that Jasper didn't have a slip. The sailboat was anchored at a mooring buoy in the harbor. It was cheaper.

"He was here one day, then was gone," Huxley said. "Still owes me rent. Son-of-a-bitch. But I'm pretty sure that's his tender tied to the dock, so maybe he's coming back. He's gonna need that."

"I don't think he's coming back," I said. "He's dead."

Huxley lifted a surprised brown. "No shit?"

"Can you show me the tender?"

He nodded and escorted me down to the dinghy dock to where the rigid inflatable was tied up.

"You're sure that's his tender?"

"Hasn't moved since he's been gone. This is where all the tenders tie up when residents that are on mooring buoys come ashore."

The pieces of the puzzle were coming together.

Jasper left his sailboat and took a tender to the dock, then caught a cab or rideshare over to Stingray Bay. I was pretty sure Jasper wasn't alive when he made it back to Pirates' Cove. My theory was that Devon ferried him back over, transferred the body aboard the *Vagabond*, tied the wake boat behind it, and headed out to sea. When he got far enough out, he scuttled the sailboat and returned to Stingray Bay.

According to the phone records, it happened after dark.

"Did you see Jasper leave the marina?"

"Not that I recall," Huxley said.

Somebody had to see something, but then again, under cover of night, who knows?

"What kind of tenant was he?"

Huxley shrugged. "He was okay. Never really caused any problems. Paid his rent, until he didn't." Huxley sighed. "But I guess I can cut him some slack since he's not breathing anymore."

"Do me a favor. Ask around. Let me know if anyone saw him leave the marina that day. There would have been another boat trailing behind him, or perhaps the other way around."

"Sounds like you suspect something."

"I think he was murdered. I just need to prove it."

Huxley seemed intrigued by the prospect of assisting. "Anything I can do to help," he assured.

I left the marina and headed back to the *Avventura* to grab JD's phone and his charger, then headed toward the hospital.

My phone buzzed with a call from Vivian. What she had to say surprised me.

"Deputy Wild, I hope I'm not disturbing you."

"Not at all," I said, the wind swirling around the cabin, the Ferrari's V8 growling.

"I talked with my husband, and he has agreed to your suggestion of bringing in another medium. He wants to settle this once and for all, and I want answers."

"I'll arrange it," I said.

"Thank you. We'll talk soon."

Now I had a problem. I had to convince the only medium I knew to do it.

38

"No, absolutely not!" Prim said.

"Why not?" I asked.

"I'm not going to open myself up to be a portal for the dead."

"I'm not asking you to really do it. Just fake it. I just need to put some pressure on this guy. Force an error."

She scoffed. "That's even worse. You want me to damage my professional reputation."

"Devon Trask murdered two people, Alaric Vesper and Jasper Armstrong."

"If you're looking for somebody to fake it, just get anybody," Prim said.

"I need someone with credibility."

"I don't understand what you're hoping to accomplish."

"It's obvious Devon killed Alaric because he worried Alaric was going to get to the truth."

"So you want to make me a target?"

"I'll be right there with you the whole time. I need him to panic more than he already has."

"The answer is still no. I know you don't believe in this stuff, but you need to at least respect it." She paused and, in a softer tone, asked, "How is everything else? I hate to admit it, but I'm a little concerned about you."

"I'm great, but JD's sick."

"JD's sick!?"

"He's in the hospital. He collapsed this morning. I think he's got the flu or something."

"It's not the flu," Prim said in a grave tone. "It's the hex."

I scoffed.

"See, this is exactly what I'm talking about. Have you given any consideration to the fact that the two might be related? Your friend all of a sudden comes down with a cold and ends up in the hospital? This is about the grimoire. I told you that book needs to be destroyed."

"JD's getting sick doesn't have anything to do with the grimoire. It has to do with him pushing himself too much, drinking too much, and bad luck."

"Bad luck because you two are messing with something that shouldn't be messed with."

I sighed, growing frustrated. "If you're not going to help, who do you recommend?"

"If you just need somebody to fake it, get one of the charla-tans on the strip. I'm sure, for a couple hundred bucks, they'll do anything you want."

"I need somebody I can trust."

"We hardly know each other. I don't think we've established trust yet."

"You came on a good referral."

There was a long pause.

I pulled into the parking lot at the hospital. "Listen, I'm at the ER. I gotta run. If you change your mind, you know how to get hold of me."

I ended the call and parked the car. A flash of my badge got me past security. I pushed through the double doors and hustled down the hallway to JD's room.

He wasn't there.

I stopped a nurse in the hall. "Did Jack Donovan get discharged?"

"No. I think the patient was admitted."

My brow lifted with concern. "Is he okay?"

"I can't discuss personal health information."

"Where's Dr. Parker?"

"I just saw him a few moments ago," she said, glancing down the hallway, scanning for him.

Parker stepped out of a patient room a moment later, and I hustled toward him. "What's the word with Jack?"

"I want to keep him overnight. His blood pressure is still low, as well as his oxygen saturation. His bloodwork came back normal. He's dehydrated, and that's likely affecting his blood pressure. Tell him to lay off the booze for a few days once he gets out." Dr. Parker sighed. "Honestly, I'm stumped. I don't know what's wrong with him, but I don't feel comfortable sending him home. I think a night of observation is the proper course. I'm sure he'll be fine, but I'd rather err on the side of caution."

I agreed.

Parker told me where I could find Jack, and I hurried through the maze of corridors.

I found JD in a room on the fifth floor. It was dim, and Jack was asleep. I took a seat in a chair beside the bed and watched the blip of his heartbeat on a monitor. The IV dripped into his arm.

I stayed there for half an hour while he slept.

A nurse darted into the room to check on him. It would be an ongoing event throughout the night. Jack peeled open his eyes and looked at me. "This is all your fault."

My face crinkled at him.

"I could be sleeping at home in my own bed."

"You could be dead."

He dismissed the notion. "They're keeping me here in an *abundance of caution*," he mocked.

"I think it's a good idea."

"I knew you would."

Brenda buzzed my phone. I pulled the device from my pocket and swiped the screen. "What have you got?"

39

"There was a little fluid in Jasper's lungs. But not as much as I would expect in a case of drowning," Brenda said. "When bodies are submerged underwater for an extended length of time, the motion can work fluid into the lungs. In my opinion, he was dead before the boat submerged."

"Any idea as to the cause of death?"

"The body is not in great shape, so it's making my job harder. But I don't see any obvious signs. I've x-rayed the body, and there are no signs of blunt-force trauma. I will run toxicology on the organ tissue and see what I find."

"Keep me posted."

"I will."

I ended the call. I filled JD in on the situation and caught him up to speed on recent events.

The nurse checked Jack's temperature and looked pleased when she read the results. "Fever's coming down a little bit. That's a good sign."

"Does that mean I can go home now?"

She laughed. "No. I'm sorry, but you're here for the duration."

JD frowned.

"You hungry?" she asked. "You think you can keep down some soft food?"

"I'm not nauseous. How about a hamburger?"

"Let me see what kind of diet your doctor has approved."

She darted out of the room.

"I guess we need to have a talk about the upcoming show," I said.

JD's brow crinkled. "What kind of talk?"

"Halloween is a few days away. I'm not sure you're going to be firing on all cylinders."

"Trust me. I'll be firing on all cylinders. Wild Fury has never canceled a show, and we're not going to start now."

"You know, there's that singer from the Royal Peasants. They did a hell of a job covering some of our songs. Maybe he could stand in."

Jack scowled at me. "Nobody stands in for me."

I laughed. "It was just a suggestion."

"Well, get that idea out of your head."

"Just take it easy and rest up so you can make the show. Do what they tell you to do and don't be difficult."

"I am never difficult," he said.

I contained myself. JD was stubborn as hell.

He was looking a little better than when we had first arrived at the ER. Still not great, but it seemed like he was bouncing back.

"Look, you don't need to stay here," he said. "You've got shit to do. Find a way to bring down Devon and figure out who killed Cassandra Ravenwood. Stop wasting time around here."

"You need anything?"

"Two blondes and a bottle of whiskey."

"I don't think they'll let me in with a bottle of whiskey, but I'll see what I can do about the blondes."

JD grinned. "Now get out of here."

"I'm gone. Call me if you need me."

I stayed a few more minutes until he threatened to have me kicked out. I left and headed back to Diver Down.

Concern tensed Teagan's face when I told her about Jack. She had a ton of questions, and I gave her the scoop on everything, including my crazy plan.

I sat at the bar, and Harlan occupied his usual position, sipping a longneck.

"Maybe Prim's right," Teagan said. "Maybe it is the hex."

I shook my head. "I'm sorry, but that's absolute nonsense. A bunch of markings on the boat aren't going to affect anybody one way or the other."

"Satanic markings. In blood!"

I rolled my eyes.

"I'm telling you, there are things out there, unknown and unexplained."

"I'm well aware of the unknown."

She paused, then a hint of a smirk tugged her plump lips. "How do you like Prim?"

"She looks pretty good for a 90-year-old."

Teagan laughed. "She looks pretty good for any age. Was she able to help you?"

I shook my head. "She hasn't exactly been cooperative. Which is why I need your help."

"My help?"

I explained my plan to her.

"Oh, hell no! I'm not getting involved."

"That's what Prim said."

"I don't blame her."

"It's just acting."

"I have no desire to be an actress. Besides, that's bad mojo."

I rolled my eyes again. "So, you're not going to help me catch a killer."

She shifted onto one hip and gave me an annoyed gaze. "Don't do that. Don't frame it like that. You know I would do anything for you."

"Anything but that."

"You're asking me to compromise my boundaries. I don't think that's fair. Besides, I helped you catch a killer before. And how did that turn out?"

I raised my hands in surrender. "Fair enough."

I ate dinner at the bar, but neither of us brought up her job offer. We were both avoiding the subject. I finally said, "About our discussion earlier. How much do you need to stay here?"

Her face wrinkled as she thought about it. "There are other perks to working for someone else. You wouldn't be my boss anymore..." She looked at me with those teal eyes, a world of possibilities in her voice.

I knew where she was going with this. We had an undeniable spark and chemistry. The employer/employee thing made it complicated, and we really hadn't gone there. I couldn't stand the thought of her leaving.

My phone buzzed with a call from Huxley, interrupting the moment. "I spoke with a guy who was moored close to Jasper's boat. You might want to hear what he has to say."

40

"Yeah, I saw him sail out of here that night," Travis said.

"You're sure about that?" I asked.

I'd hustled over to Pirates' Cove to speak with him. We stood on the dock with Huxley. Water lapped against hulls, the stars flickered overhead, and a gentle breeze drifted through the marina.

Travis was late 50s with brown hair that had more gray in it than its original color. He kept himself in good shape. He had hazel eyes, a sun-weathered face, and wore glasses.

"Positive," Travis said. "Some guy in a small wake boat dropped him off. Jasper weighed anchor, fired up the diesel, then navigated out of the marina. I thought he was just going out for an evening cruise, but he never came back."

"Where were you when you saw Jasper?" I asked.

"I had gone to Oyster Avenue for dinner and drinks and came back to the marina. I was right there," he pointed, "boarding my tender."

The distance from the dock to Jasper's sailboat was about 50 yards.

"Are you sure it was Jasper?" I asked again.

"I'd bet my life on it. Good-looking young kid."

"Can you describe the wake boat?"

"White with a metallic red accent on the side."

It matched the description of Devon's boat.

I thanked Travis for his cooperation and gave him a card. I told him to get in touch if he remembered any additional details.

"Jasper is really dead, huh?"

I nodded.

"That's a shame. Seemed like a nice kid."

I said goodbye to Travis and Huxley and hustled back to the parking lot, hopped into the Ferrari, and drove to the *Avventura*. This new information didn't exactly jive with my theory and wouldn't help with my case against Devon.

Teagan called as I walked down the dock toward the superyacht. She must have seen me pull into the parking lot or heard the roar of the engine. It was unmistakable. "Ok. I'm in. I'll do the fake séance. On one condition."

"What's the condition?"

"When this is all said and done, I want us all to go on vacation. Someplace fun and relaxing where you guys don't have to solve crimes, and we can all just recharge. You guys work too hard and look where it's gotten JD. I'm scared. I worry about you two. Both of you burn the candle at both ends and act like you're invincible." Her voice was soft and heartfelt.

It was touching.

"Okay. A vacation it is."

"And you never ask me to use my psychic powers again."

"Deal."

"When are we doing this?"

"As soon as I can set it up."

She paused. "And I want a new job title."

"Okay. What do you want to be called? Drink Service Engineer? Chief Mixologist?"

"Manager. I like the sound of that. It's what I do anyway."

"Deal."

"And with that comes a managerial salary."

"What do you have in mind?"

"I'm gonna throw a number out there. It's a big number, but you can handle it because both of you are loaded."

I laughed.

I wasn't laughing when she spit out the number. But it was fair. She was worth more than that. In the spirit of good fun,

I delayed my response.

"So, what do you think?" she asked.

"I think you didn't ask for enough."

"I can ask for more," she said with a smile in her voice.

I countered with a number that was even higher. "I don't want you getting any funny ideas about going to another bar. I like you right where you are."

"I don't have any funny ideas."

"With the new title comes more responsibility."

She laughed. "How much more responsibility can I take on?"

"You're in charge of everything. Supplies, entertainment, advertising, staffing. You're going to run the show."

"Boss Bitch. I like it."

I chuckled. "Is that your new title? Do you want it on business cards?"

Teagan was one of the kindest, gentlest, most agreeable people I knew. The title Boss Bitch didn't really suit her, but she seemed to enjoy the moniker.

"Sure. Why not?"

"I'll see what I can do."

I had no sooner ended the call when Prim rang. The two girls were in sync.

"Okay. I'll do it. On one condition," Prim said.

I laughed. "Actually, you're off the hook. Teagan agreed to do it."

"But that's not her thing. She's not a medium." There was a hint of jealousy in Prim's voice.

"Like I said, all I need to do is rattle Devon's cage. I'm not exactly sure what's going on. New evidence has come to light."

"What new evidence?"

I told her what Travis had said.

"I think this is over Teagan's head. You need professional help."

I laughed again. "I've been told that before."

"No. I'm serious."

"Why the change of heart?"

"I don't know. Call it a feeling. Intuition. Gut instinct. Besides, you came to my aid when I needed you. It seems only fair."

"I appreciate the offer."

"How's Jack?"

Only JD's close friends called him Jack. It was an interesting choice for her to use. "They're keeping him overnight. I think he's making progress."

"What are you doing to find the grimoire?"

"Everything I can, but it's not enough."

She hesitated for a moment. "I may be able to help."

"How so?" "

"I helped find it before. I can try again."

"I thought you said it's being concealed?"

"It is. But after my last experience, I didn't try too hard."

"I thought you didn't want to open yourself up to that kind of energy."

"If you're not part of the solution, you're part of the problem, right?"

"Something like that," I said.

"But I may need a small favor."

"Anything."

"I have not been able to get a contractor out to fix my window. My friend that I'm staying with has family coming in later tonight and needs the room."

"You need a place to stay?"

"No. I'm fully capable of getting myself a hotel room if need be. But I thought, if you're handy with a set of tools, maybe you might be able to replace the window?"

"The hardware stores are closed now, but I'd be happy to see what I can do tomorrow."

"I guess I'll just see if there's a place available at the Coconut Cottage."

"You're not gonna find a vacancy this time of year."

The island was packed for Halloween. Tourists from all over flock to the island for the festivities and the horror convention.

"I have spare guest rooms," I said, just throwing it out there.

41

"What are you doing?" I asked.

"It's sage," Prim said as she lit the spice and waved it in the air. She walked through the salon, wisps of smoke drifting in her wake. "This place needs to be cleansed of evil spirits. Especially after that hex."

"Maybe you should have done that sooner."

"You didn't ask."

"Want something to drink?"

She considered it as she continued throughout the boat. "I'll take a margarita."

"One margarita, coming right up," I said.

I slipped behind the bar and shouted, "Frozen? Salt?"

"Yes, to both." Her voice rang out, echoing from a forward passage.

I grabbed a packet of margarita mix, poured it into the blender, tossed in all the requisite elements, then pulverized the ingredients. The ice rattled in the industrial-strength device, and within moments, I had whipped up a frozen slush of tropical bliss.

I grabbed the margarita glass, rimmed it with salt, poured the beverage, and waited for her return.

Prim left no part of the boat unexplored. I don't think she wanted to take any chances after the hex, and I couldn't blame her.

She stepped back into the salon several minutes later with trails of smoke. She extinguished the spice and joined me at the bar. I handed her the frozen delight, and she smiled with appreciation. "Thank you."

She took a sip and tasted the high-octane tequila. Judging by her reaction, it may have been a little stout. "You're not playing around."

"If you're gonna make a drink, make a drink."

"Are you trying to get me drunk?"

"I would do no such thing."

She gave me a doubtful glance.

"Relax. That's the only one you get."

"What if I want more?"

"You'll have to make it yourself. I'm off duty. Bar's closed."

She scoffed. "I get the impression that the bar never closes around here."

"Shall we take our drinks to the sky deck?"

"Why not?"

I escorted her from the salon, and we sat in lounge chairs on the sky deck and looked up at the stars while we sipped our beverages.

"You know, this is a nice boat."

"It gets the job done."

She laughed. "And what job is that? Full-time hedonism?"

"We give it our best shot." I smiled.

"I have no doubt." She paused. "Just so we're clear, I appreciate your hospitality, but I hope you're not expecting anything in return."

I smiled. "I have no expectations. I told you, you're not my type."

Her blue eyes gave me a doubtful glance. "You forget I'm clairvoyant."

I stared back at her. "What am I thinking right now?"

"I can't say without blushing." She blushed a little.

She was probably right. She looked gorgeous. Prim was a little kooky, but I could deal with kooky for a few days. Maybe longer.

We continued to stare at each other for another moment.

"You're thinking about your friend," she said. "You're worried."

"Of course, I'm worried. He's my best friend. I've never seen him this sick before."

"I know you don't believe it, but that book must be destroyed. That's the only way to help your friend. And there's only one way to do it."

I played along. "How?"

"First, we must find it. The person in possession of the book will show outward signs."

"How so?"

"The book giveth, and the book taketh away. Wealth, power, status, beauty, longevity. All of those are benefits that will be passed to the owner for a time. But it's not without its price, and the book will collect. It always collects."

I still regarded the whole thing with disbelief. "Can we focus on more tangible subjects? I think I'm all spooked out for the evening."

"What would you like to talk about?"

"What have you got against cops?"

"Maybe that's something I don't really want to talk about."

"We're not all bad," I said.

"I see that. I also see a lot of corruption. Especially in Pineapple Bay."

"This isn't Pineapple Bay."

She gave me a knowing glance. "But this town has its fair share. Politicians on the take, corrupt judges, dirty cops."

"Our department is pretty clean," I said, getting defensive. Most of the guys I knew on the force were good men.

"Please, Paris Delaney finds out everything that's going on in this town. She's paying someone in the department. You know that."

"I'm aware. Do you know what it's like to live on a cop's salary?"

"Are you making excuses?"

"I'm not making excuses for anybody."

She stared at me for a long moment.

"If you don't want to talk about it, that's fine. We can talk about something else."

She hesitated. "I grew up in Pineapple Bay. From an early age, I always knew I was a little different. I had a gift. My mother didn't have it, but my grandmother did. She helped me discover it." She paused. "My older brother, Rowan, was like you. He didn't believe." Her tone grew somber. "He got picked up by the Pineapple Bay PD. Wrong place, wrong time. I warned him, but he didn't listen. He was 19 at the time and had been out drinking at a party. Rowan did the right thing. He left his car behind and walked home. He cut through the Ocean Crest Estates. Apparently, there had been a break-in. Rowan was put in a lineup, and a witness fingered him as the burglar. As I'm sure you know, Ocean Crest is an upscale neighborhood. There was a lot of pressure on the Pineapple Bay Police Department to close the case and send a message. They planted evidence on my brother."

"You know that for a fact?"

Prim clenched her jaw. "My brother would never break into a house. He had no criminal history. He wouldn't steal. It was total bullshit. I got visions of the case, and I tried to assist the police department in tracking down the real burglars. They completely dismissed me. They wouldn't listen. They had my brother in custody. They had fabricated evidence, and they weren't going to change their story. If they changed their story, the truth would have come out, and they'd have been exposed. My brother was sentenced to 15 years. Rowan was a good kid. He had a full scholarship and his whole life ahead of him. All that was taken away because he did the right thing and walked home that summer night." Prim's eyes misted. "He killed himself after six weeks in jail."

That hung there like smoke.

"I'm sorry."

She wiped the tears from her eyes. "So, you will forgive me if I have a little mistrust of the system."

"Understandable." I paused. "We can go back to talking about spooky stuff now."

She chuckled. "Too real for you?"

"I can assure you, my partner and I have never planted evidence on a suspect."

"What about the people you know are guilty but you can't prove?"

I gave her a knowing glance. "Let's just say sometimes fate takes care of those people."

She lifted her curious brow. "Are you often the hand of fate?"

I smiled. "I work within the confines of the law."

It was true, for the most part.

I was trying not to kill people unless it was absolutely justified. It would have been easy, in a lot of situations, to go pure vigilante. But I was trying to stay on the right side of things.

"Perhaps I shouldn't ask any more questions," she said.

"Perhaps."

She finished the last of her margarita and dangled the empty glass in front of me. "I think I need a refill."

"I told you I was only making you one. You might be on the floor after two."

She gave me a sassy look. "I can handle my liquor. I'm an adult, and if I want two drinks, I can have two drinks. Besides, what do you think is going to happen? One more margarita, and I'll involuntarily throw myself at you?"

"I don't know. How much self-control do you have?"

She sneered at me playfully. "I have plenty of self-control."

I took her glass and moved to the bar on the sky deck. I whipped her up another margarita. This time I went light on the tequila, then poured myself another glass of whiskey. Just as I returned and handed her the glass, my phone buzzed with a call from the sheriff.

I really didn't want to pick it up.

42

"**G**ood news for a change," the sheriff said. "That dagger turned up. Some nitwit in property misplaced it."

"That's good news."

"The better news... The lab got a match on a print. Caspian Blackstone. He was in the system on a prior arrest."

I grinned.

"Go get that son-of-a-bitch."

"I'm kind of in the middle of something."

"I don't care who she is. I want you and that numbskull partner of yours to go arrest him."

I winced. "JD's in the hospital."

"What!?"

I caught him up to speed.

"Is he okay?"

"If he was okay, he wouldn't be in the hospital," I said.

Daniels took a solemn pause. "Do I need to be worried about him?"

"I'm sure he's fine. He just came down with the flu or something," I said, trying to convince myself.

"You keep me updated on his situation. Does he need anything?"

"I got him covered."

"I know that you do. Where are you now?"

"On the boat."

"If you want to sit this one out, I understand."

"No. I'm there." I ended the call and slipped the phone back into my pocket. I told my temporary houseguest that I had to run. "Duty calls."

She frowned. "And here I was, thinking I might lose control."

I smiled. "Feel free to lose control when I return."

She smirked. "You wish."

"Make yourself at home. I don't know when I'll be back."

"Be safe," she added.

"Always." That wasn't exactly the truth. There's nothing safe about this job.

I met Erickson, Faulkner, Robinson, and Mendoza at the station. There were lots of questions about JD, and I told them the situation. We all gave each other a lot of hell, but when it came down to it, these guys would take a bullet for anybody on the team. They all wished JD well and said they'd call and harass him soon.

I hopped into the back of the patrol car with Erickson and Faulkner, and we cruised over to the Trident Tower. I suited up in a tactical vest and press-checked my weapon. Adrenaline coursed through my veins. I didn't anticipate Caspian would give us much trouble, but I was prepared for anything.

The squad cars pulled under the carport, and we flooded out of the vehicles. I flashed my badge, and the concierge buzzed us in. We stormed into the lobby.

The night concierge looked stunned, her eyes wide.

"We've got a warrant," I said. "Can you let us into Caspian Blackstone's condo, or do we need to break down the door?"

"Have you tried knocking first?" she asked in a slightly sarcastic tone.

Within minutes, the squad was standing outside of Caspian's door. I banged a heavy fist, and shouted, "Coconut County! We have a warrant!"

There was no response.

The concierge slipped the key card into the slot, and I flung open the door. She stepped aside as we flooded into the condo.

I shouted again, "Sheriff's Department. We have a warrant."

With weapons drawn, we filed down the hallway into the living room.

It was a nice place with open architecture. An expansive living room that opened to a large terrace. Floor-to-ceiling windows offered a view of the ocean. There were two bedrooms downstairs, one on either side of the condo. Stairs led up to a second floor with two more guest bedrooms. It was one of the larger units in the building.

Caspian stood in a panic near the terrace. In a dramatic gesture, he threw something to the ground, then disappeared in a cloud of smoke.

I should have expected nothing less from a supposed warlock.

The fog filled the living room, and I darted through the soupy haze onto the balcony. It was clearly a misdirection tactic. As I emerged into the clear air of the terrace, Caspian was gone.

I knew he wasn't gifted with magical capabilities.

He had to be here somewhere.

I rushed to the edge of the terrace and peered over.

Caspian had climbed over the balcony and lowered himself down. He dangled, his fingers gripping the ledge. I knew he was trying to swing down onto the balcony below, but he was 27 stories in the air.

It was a long way down, and there were gusts of wind.

The average person can't hang by their fingertips for very long. They overestimate their strength.

I leaned over the railing and shouted at him, "There's nowhere to go."

He looked up at me with panicked eyes.

Caspian quickly realized this was perhaps one of the dumbest things he'd ever done. If he wasn't careful, it was going to be the last thing he ever did.

43

C aspian rocked his legs back and forth, gaining momentum. His feet swung out, then in, then he let go.

I gave it 50-50 whether he would make it onto the balcony below, threading the narrow gap. There was a chance that he'd make it halfway and break his back on the railing below.

Caspian tumbled to the lower balcony, sprang to his feet, and sprinted into the residence.

We hustled through the condo and spilled into the hallway. I raced down the corridor, sprinting toward the stairwell while Mendoza and Robinson took the elevator.

I burst through the steel fire door and spiraled down to the level below, then charged into the hallway.

Caspian sprinted toward the elevator.

The door slid open, and Mendoza and Robinson waited for the perp with triumphant grins.

Caspian skidded to a halt, then headed back in the opposite direction toward me for a few steps, then froze.

He contemplated his options for a moment, but there weren't any. Finally, he raised his hands in surrender.

"On the ground, now!" I shouted. "Hands behind your head."

He got on the ground and complied.

Mendoza and Robinson raced forward and ratcheted the cuffs around his wrists. They pulled him to his feet and escorted him to the elevator.

"Caspian Blackstone, you're under arrest for the murder of Cassandra Ravenwood," Mendoza said. "You have the right to remain silent…"

Mendoza and Robinson escorted him down to the lobby while Erickson, Faulkner, and I went back to his condo and searched the premises for the Obsidian Codex.

We turned the place upside down, rooting through bookshelves, dresser drawers, closets. We looked under the mattress and in pillowcases. We scoured every nook and cranny but didn't find the grimoire.

At the station, I filled out after-action reports, then paid the scumbag a little visit.

I stepped into the interrogation room and took a seat across the table from him. "You're lucky you're not a grease spot. That was a pretty crazy stunt you pulled. I've seen people try it before and not make it."

"What can I say? The gods were looking after me."

"Doesn't really seem that way. Here you are, looking at a capital murder charge."

He frowned.

"You're a relatively young guy. That's a long time to spend behind bars. Maybe a grease spot would have been a better option."

"I'm innocent," he said.

I stifled a chuckle. "That's a good one. Why did you run?"

"I panicked."

"Innocent people don't run."

"I wasn't certain what your intentions were."

I laughed. "My intentions were to arrest you and bring you to justice."

"You have to understand that I receive all kinds of threats. People want what I have."

"What do you have?"

"Various valuable items. Talismans, amulets, magical daggers. I can't trust anyone." He paused. "I'm assuming my apartment was left wide open, allowing anyone to plunder my possessions."

"We locked up before we left. You're lucky you still have a front door. Speaking of daggers, care to explain why your fingerprints were on the dagger that killed Cassandra Ravenwood?"

His jaw tightened. "I didn't kill her." He said in a slow, deliberate voice, his eyes focused on mine. "I approached her the day of her death, requesting the grimoire once again. I tried to impress upon her how dangerous it was and the urgency required for proper action. She pulled the dagger on me in self-defense."

"You assaulted her?"

"No. But she clearly felt intimidated. I grabbed her hand, and she jerked the blade free, cutting my palm."

His hands were cuffed to his waist, and he lifted them to display the gash that had started to scab over.

"So that's how your fingerprint got on the dagger?"

"I would assume so. I also assume you'll find my blood on that dagger."

"Where's the Obsidian Codex?"

The muscles in his jaw flexed. "I told you, I don't have it. Cassandra wouldn't give it to me."

"Are you sure you didn't take it?"

"No."

I lifted a curious brow. "No, you're not sure?"

"No, I didn't take it."

I didn't believe him, and I was growing tired of this nonsense. "You expect me to believe that your fingerprints, and potentially your blood, are on the dagger that killed Cassandra, but you didn't stab her? Add to that the fact that you did your best to avoid capture. It makes me suspicious."

"I don't care what you believe. I know the truth."

I leaned into the table and stared him down. "My friend is in the hospital right now. I don't know if it has anything to do with that damn book or not. But I'm not leaving this room until you tell me where it is. Now, we can do this the easy way, or we can do it the hard way."

"I want to speak with an attorney," he said in a smug tone.

Those were the magic words. I had to stop questioning him.

"I'm sorry I didn't hear you," I said.

He repeated the request.

I shook my head. "Nope. Still not able to understand. You're mumbling. Now I'm going to give you one more opportunity to tell me where the grimoire is, or things are going to get ugly."

The gloves were about to come off, and I had thoughts of crossing a line.

44

D aniels poked his head into the interrogation room. "Wild, get out here. Now!"

I frowned and pushed away from the table. The chair screeched, and I marched out of the room. I had a little conference with Daniels in the hallway.

"I don't know if you're aware, but when he asks for an attorney, you have to stop the interrogation," he snarked.

"That bastard knows exactly where that grimoire is," I said.

"Who cares? It's just a book. You're not starting to believe this shit, are you?"

"No."

"I know you're worried about JD," he said in a compassionate tone. "We all are. But the last thing any of us need is you flying off the handle and using *enhanced* interrogation tactics on that scumbag."

"I wasn't going to beat him to a pulp."

"I saw that look in your eyes."

"I was just trying to intimidate him," I said, downplaying it with an innocent shrug.

"Go home. Relax. Clear your head. Go back to that lady friend of yours. JD's gonna be just fine, and the case will still be here tomorrow."

He patted me on the shoulder before marching away.

I left the station and headed back to Diver Down. It was late by the time I boarded the boat, and all was quiet.

Buddy trotted down the steps and into the salon to greet me. I knelt down and petted the little guy, took him out for a walk, then returned to the boat.

A nice surprise waited for me in my stateroom. Prim was curled up in my bed, snuggling a pillow. She peeled open her sleepy eyes when I entered. "This bed is so much more comfortable than the one below deck. You don't mind, do you?"

I tried to contain my enthusiasm. "No. I don't mind at all."

"I didn't figure you would." She paused. "Did you get your man?"

"I did."

"Did you find the grimoire?"

"I didn't."

She frowned. "That's odd. Caspian likes to think of himself as a protector. He wouldn't let it out of his sight."

"Well, we left no stone unturned in his condo. It wasn't there."

"Go back and look again."

"I will."

"In the meantime, you're wearing entirely too much." With a devious sparkle in her eyes, she pulled back the covers, revealing her svelte form—smooth skin, supple curves, toned thighs, buoyant assets. She was a slice of heaven, and I was ready to indulge.

"I guess I have an impulse control problem after all," she said.

"Did you have that second margarita?"

"No, but that would be a convenient excuse. Life is short. Why deny ourselves a simple pleasure?"

"I wholeheartedly agree."

"Besides, this was inevitable. I knew this was going to happen the first time I saw you in the parking lot. Though I couldn't exactly figure out how all the pieces were going to fit together."

I peeled out of my clothes and slipped under the covers with her. My pulse pounded, and the flames of desire burned. Our lips collided, and our bodies intertwined. We got acquainted with one another, and my hands explored her smooth skin, soft peaks, and delightful valleys. Our tongues danced, and heat radiated between us.

She gasped with pleasure as the puzzle pieces fit together. Her breathy moans tickled my ear, and her nails dug into my back for an instant.

We tumbled around the sheets and worked up a helluva sweat. It didn't take a clairvoyant to see how this was going to end. This had been brewing from the first moment I saw her at Waffle Wizard. I still hadn't satiated my desire for blueberry waffles, but this was an even better treat.

Slick with desire, we crescendoed in a mad, passionate explosion of pleasure chemicals. It was, dare I say, magical.

We collapsed beside each other, catching our breath, basking in the afterglow.

She nuzzled close and stroked my skin. "I feel a lot less stressed out."

"That was a nice distraction," I said.

"Yes, it was. We might have to get distracted again."

I couldn't agree more.

I passed out in a state of heady bliss, the gorgeous blonde snuggling beside me all night.

It was a good way to end the evening, but the morning brought woe.

45

My phone buzzed with a call from Dr. Parker. "Well, I hate to make this phone call."

My heart sank the instant he said that. "What's going on? Is he okay?"

My voice trembled slightly, and my throat tightened. It seemed like an eternity before I got an answer, and when I did, I didn't like it.

"JD took a turn last night. He went into respiratory failure and slipped into a coma. We've got him on a ventilator and broad-spectrum antibiotics. And also on a vasosuppressor to help maintain blood pressure. I suspect this is some kind of septic shock. The offending organism was missed on the initial blood work, but we sent additional labs out for culture. I should know shortly exactly what we're dealing with. Could be some type of toxic shock syndrome. I'm just not sure. Honestly, I'm scratching my head a little. I wish I had more answers for you. His immune system may have been weakened by a night of heavy drinking. It's hard to say."

My throat was so tight I could hardly speak. "What's the prognosis? What are we looking at?"

"I've known you two long enough that I'm not going to pull any punches. It's not looking good. Hope for the best, prepare for the worst. I know he's got a daughter out in California. She might want to come see him. Could be the last time."

I tried to hold back the mists that brimmed my eyes, but that was difficult to do. "Thanks for the update. Keep me posted."

I ended the call and sat there on the edge of the bed, dazed for a moment.

Prim put a comforting hand on my back. "Is everything okay?"

I shook my head, unable to speak.

I took a moment to process the situation and pull myself together. JD was strong, and he wasn't going to go out without a fight. That gave me a little hope.

My next call was to Scarlett. I filled her in on the situation. She burst into tears, and I did my best to put a positive spin on it.

"I'll be on the next plane," she said, sniffling through tears.

"You know Jack. This isn't the way he's going out."

She sniffled again. "I know."

"Let me know as soon as you've got your travel arrangements made. I'll pick you up from the airport. You can stay aboard the boat."

"Thanks, Tyson. Keep me posted."

"I will."

I showered, dressed, and made a trip to the hospital with Prim. We walked through the seafoam green hallways in the intensive care unit and found Jack's room. My skin tingled with nerves, and that sense of dread twisted my gut. I didn't want to see Jack like this. It was hard.

The ventilator clicked and wheezed, and the monitor beside the bed displayed vitals. The jagged peaks of his heart rose and fell.

I stood beside the bed, took his hand, and squeezed tight. "You're gonna be okay, buddy."

It was hard to get the words out. My voice was on the verge of cracking.

There was no response. But I had to believe he heard me.

"You're gonna get through this, and we're gonna be back to our old shenanigans in no time. Don't tell anybody, but I snuck in whiskey and a blonde. You're missing out."

Even *that* didn't get a response.

I called the guys in the band and told them the bad news. It didn't take them long to show up at the hospital. The trio spilled into the room and looked at JD with mortified eyes. They asked a bunch of questions, and I answered them as best as I could. But nobody really had any answers.

I introduced the gang to Prim.

They all wished Jack well and talked about all the gigs and parties that we were going to have once he got out. They told tall tales of future exploits, mega rock stardom, and sultry encounters with adventurous groupies.

It was good for him to know that we were all here and that we all loved him.

I told the guys I'd cancel the show and find a replacement.

"The show is the least of our worries," Crash said.

"He wouldn't want us to cancel the show," Styxx said.

"There is no Wild Fury without Thrash," Crash replied. It was Jack's stage name.

"We could do a tribute show," Dizzy said.

Crash shook his head. "I don't know. It just wouldn't feel right. Besides, there's no need for a tribute show. He's gonna get up and walk out of here in time to sing on stage." The tears spilled over his lids by the time he finished.

We all agreed that Jack would make a full recovery.

Maybe, just maybe, The Universe would listen to our demands.

46

S carlett stepped off the sleek slipstream G-750, wearing a pink baseball cap, oversized sunglasses, and her hair pulled back. She wore blue jeans and a white T-shirt and had a small pink carry-on in tow. At a casual glance, you wouldn't know who she was.

In Los Angeles, her picture was all over billboards, benches, and the sides of buses. She was one of the biggest movie stars on the planet, and her superhero franchise had topped box office charts over the summer. Scarlett's meteoric rise to stardom was nothing short of miraculous. Some people toil for years in Los Angeles and never catch a break. It happened overnight for Scarlett, and despite her tumultuous past, she seemed to be handling it well.

The private jet gleamed in the brilliant Florida sun.

I waited on the tarmac for her.

Scarlett plummeted down the steps and gave me a tight hug. We stood there, silent as we held a long embrace.

"I'm so scared," she finally whispered.

"I know. Me too."

"Why is this happening?"

"I don't know. They're still running tests, trying to figure it out."

She lifted her sunglasses and wiped the tears from her eyes.

I grabbed her roller case and escorted her through the terminal at the FBO.

A striking redhead approached hand in hand with her boyfriend. I didn't recognize her at first. She was positively radiant.

"Gwen?"

She looked at me, and it took an instant to register. "Deputy Wild!" What are you doing here?"

"Picking up a friend. You?"

She smiled. "Day trip to the Bahamas."

"Sounds like fun," I said, making small talk.

"Oh, this is my boyfriend, Sebastian."

We shook hands, and I introduced them to Scarlett. Surprisingly, they didn't make the connection. I don't think they were expecting to run into a movie star. Gwen was too smitten with her beau to think about anything else.

She looked better than I remembered. I figured she'd gotten a facial, some Botox, and maybe some filler.

"You got back together?" I said, surprised.

Gwen smiled. "It seems destiny can't keep us apart."

She gave him an adoring smile, and he smiled back.

"How's the investigation?" she asked.

"We're making progress. Minor setback. My partner's taken ill. We're just on the way to the hospital to see him."

Her face wrinkled with concern. "Oh, no! Is he okay?"

I shrugged.

Scarlett tried to hold it together.

Gwen could tell the situation was grave. She rushed forward and hugged me tight. "I'm so sorry. I'll keep you both in my prayers."

"Thank you. It's much appreciated."

There was an awkward pause after she broke away.

"Well, enjoy your trip," I said.

She smiled again. "We will. And send my best to your partner."

We continued on, and they took a seat near the window, waiting on their plane.

"What was that all about?" Scarlett asked.

I told her about the recent cases, and she looked at me with disbelief at some of the weird happenings.

I escorted Scarlett out to the parking lot, took her bag, and stuffed it into the front trunk. I grabbed her door, then hustled around, hopped behind the wheel, and cranked up the Ferrari.

"Nice ride," she said with an impressed face.

"Logan Chase gave it to me."

"I heard."

We zipped toward the hospital, the wind swirling around the open top.

"So, how are things?" I asked, trying to add a degree of normalcy to the situation.

"Other than this, everything is great. Sorry to hear about the TV show."

"It's not dead," I said. "Just rescheduled. Everything got thrown for a loop."

We were supposed to go into production of a TV show based on our adventures. The mishap with Logan Chase and Brad Tyler had put the project into limbo. Now it was a matter of working it back into the stars' busy schedules. The studio had expressed concern about filming the project in Coconut Key as originally planned. As it stood, they weren't about to let those two movie stars out of their sight. They wanted to keep them on a short leash and shoot the production in and around Los Angeles. I'm not exactly sure how they would pull it off, but I guess from the right angles and with a little Hollywood magic, they could make California look like Florida.

Maybe.

It was the least of my concerns at the moment.

We pulled into the lot at the hospital, and I escorted Scarlett to JD's room. She trembled by the time we entered. Tears streamed behind those glasses as she stepped into the room and saw him for the first time. She pulled off the shades and wiped her eyes, and I put my arm around her.

"Hey, Scarlett," Crash said. "Really sorry about your dad. He's going to be okay, though."

She sniffled, nodded, then moved to his bedside. She took his hand and told him she loved him.

Brenda buzzed my phone.

I stepped into the hallway to take the call. "What have you got?"

"There was a red hair tangled around the dagger."

"Cassandra's?"

"That was my thought at first, but I compared the two. I'm reasonably certain this hair did not come from Cassandra. Unfortunately, this is a broken strand, and there is no follicle, so it will make it more difficult to DNA type. But I've done a chemical analysis on Cassandra's hair and this strand. They are coated in different chemical compounds. Different shampoos and conditioners."

It all came together in my mind. "You know who else has red hair."

"You're the investigator. You tell me."

"Her sister, Gwen."

"Can you get a hair sample?"

"I can," I said, a scheme brewing in my mind.

I glanced at my shirt, hoping a strand of hair had transferred to the fabric when she hugged me.

No such luck.

We didn't have enough evidence at this point to get a warrant to compel Gwen to hand over a strand of hair. I'd have to acquire it another way.

Gwen had multiple reasons to kill her sister.

I told Brenda I'd be in touch, ended the call, and slipped my phone into my pocket. I poked my head back into the room and told Scarlett and the guys that I had to run.

Scarlett understood. "I'm going to stay here. I'll probably spend the night with him."

"Keep in touch. Let me know if you need anything—food, water, whatever."

"My bag from the car," she said.

I nodded, hustled down to the parking lot, grabbed her bag, and returned to the room.

I had a crazy idea in mind. It was insane, stupid, reckless, and highly illegal. But desperate times call for desperate measures. I had a limited window of opportunity, and time was of the essence. I gave it some consideration and thought WWJDD—what would JD do?

47

I wouldn't normally do this kind of thing. It went against my *by-the-book* ethos. But this was an unusual circumstance, and I figured I could kill two birds with one stone.

I stood in front of Gwen's apartment wearing overalls, a cheap latex mask with a spooky pale face, and wild hair. A kitchen knife dangled from my grasp. My hands were gloved in latex. I looked like a serial killer from a slasher movie. This time of year, no one would think twice about it.

The sun had dipped over the horizon, and I had seen others wandering about the complex in costume. Tomorrow night was the big night, but parties were happening all over the island leading up to the hallowed eve.

JD wouldn't hesitate. He'd pick the lock, search the apartment, take a strand of hair from a hairbrush, and say it transferred onto his shirt when the perp hugged him. At least, that's what he'd *want* to do.

I glanced around to make sure nobody was watching. There were no video cameras around, and I certainly hadn't driven my Ferrari to the property.

I sat there for a moment, contemplating how far I would go. Would I cross an ethical line? My friend was dying in the hospital. I didn't really believe in intangible things, but by the same token, I didn't want to leave anything to chance. Odds were good the grimoire was in this apartment. Gwen was on a day trip and wouldn't be back anytime soon. Now was the chance.

With a simple lock-picking kit, I was in the door in no time. I slipped inside, closed the door behind me, and locked it.

I advanced into the living room and pushed through the door to the bedroom. The slits for eyeholes in the mask didn't offer much in the way of vision. The latex was hot against my skin, and my face was slick with sweat. I pulled off the mask and took a breath of air. The restricted disguise induced an overload of CO_2.

In the master bath, it was easy to find a strand of hair around the drain. Gwen had taken her hairbrush on vacation.

I collected a few samples, bagged the evidence, and stuffed it into my pocket.

I hadn't made up my mind what I was going to do with it. Would I submit it as evidence and claim it transferred onto my shirt during our encounter at the FBO? Or would I just have Brenda positively match it so I knew where to focus my attention?

I left the bathroom and continued to search the apartment for the grimoire.

Doubt crept into my mind, and I thought that I had lost it for a moment. This was completely out of bounds, inappropriate, unethical. What was I doing? There was no explaining something like this. No justifying it. It was pure madness. *"Well, you see, Your Honor, I believed this book was magical and causing my friend's death."*

That wouldn't fly.

I scanned the bookshelves, rummaged through dresser drawers, and searched the closet.

Inside was a small metal safe.

It was a digital combination locking safe with a backup key. Steel construction with large locking bolts—a California-DOJ certified gun safe for firearm storage. The dimensions were roughly 16 x 14 x 9. It weighed about 25 pounds. These kinds of safes were relatively cheap and effective, to a degree. They kept nosy people out of your belongings.

But this wasn't Fort Knox.

There were three LED lights above the keypad. A fatal flaw in the design. The lights were held in place on a circuit board that was glued to a sponge attached to the back of the keypad. I'd run into this kind of safe before. You could get one at any home improvement store or online. I grabbed a coat hanger, poked it through one of the LED holes, and displaced the circuit board. It was easy to do. Then I removed the coat hanger, flipped it around to the hook side, and threaded it through the LED hole. I used it to actuate the solenoid.

The locking mechanism released.

I twisted the handle and opened the door.

Child's play.

The evil book rested inside. The object of relentless pursuit. Bound in leather by hand and printed on parchment, it looked ancient.

It was with a mix of anticipation and trepidation that I pulled it from the safe. I admired the legendary grimoire for a moment. It was, supposedly, the very essence of evil itself. The obsidian black cover was embossed with a solitary inverted pentagram.

I was almost disappointed. I expected more fanfare—a cold draft, whispering spirits, a feeling of malevolence.

I experienced none of those things.

It was just a book.

Still, I couldn't resist the temptation to open it and thumb through the pages. Scrawled in blood were various incantations, spells, and sigils. The letters swooped and swirled with expert penmanship, drafted with skill and care, yet lacking the perfection of mass-printed material. It had texture and character. A macabre symphony of calligraphy. I could see why a collector would want such a piece.

The book smelled old—a pungent aroma of must and decay. The pages were weathered and worn, stained with the oil of a thousand fingers that had tabbed through the incantations. Whispered words of forbidden tongues, sinister spells to bend the will of others, invocations to summon infernal creatures from the depths of hell. If you wanted to conjure the devil himself, this book could show you how. At least, that's what some believed.

The blood had darkened but still had a rust-colored tint. I didn't want to know whose blood was on these pages. Perhaps a virgin sacrifice. Perhaps many. Perhaps the author's. The words pulsed with dark energy. A sinister dance of the sacrilegious and profane. A compendium of forbidden power.

It was creepy to read, but I found myself entranced by each page. It was a masterpiece of the macabre. Such care and concern had gone into the crafting of the book. It made it fascinating and horrific. The pages seemed to live and breathe. I could see how its malevolent aura could ensnare someone who believed in that kind of thing.

I'm not sure how much time passed as I examined the book in the closet. It was like nothing else in the world existed.

When I finally closed the book and stepped out of the closet, I realized my error. The book's intrigue had distracted me so much that I didn't notice Gwen had returned. She stood in the bedroom near the doorway, a semiautomatic pistol aimed at me.

It was a perfectly legitimate response to seeing a strange man dressed as a serial killer in your bedroom. I couldn't blame her.

I began to think this was a terrible idea.

"You're back," I said casually with a smile.

"Mechanical difficulties," she muttered.

Gwen didn't wait for an explanation. She squeezed the trigger. Muzzle flash flickered, and the bullet rocketed from the barrel. Smoke wafted, and the deafening sound echoed off the walls.

48

The impact was like a sledgehammer to the chest. It forced all the air out of my lungs and knocked me to the ground. My chest ached, and I gasped for breath. The sharp pain in my sternum radiated through my entire body.

She had every right to shoot me.

For a moment, I thought this was the end of my second chance. I braced mentally for the journey into the unknown. This time, where would I go? Up or down? Heaven or Hell? Maybe somewhere in between.

I thought about my legacy. What would I leave behind? The headline would read: *Deputy shot dead while breaking and entering.*

Paris would have a field day.

It took me a second to realize I wasn't dead or dying. Gwen's bullet had hit the Codex that I held before me, and the Codex smacked into my chest.

I tried to suck in a breath of air but couldn't.

Gwen advanced, determination in her eyes. This was her opportunity. A free pass to put as many bullets into me as would do the job. After all, I had no legal right to be here. Sure, I could argue exigent circumstances, but that wouldn't hold water. Not in this case.

She hovered over me, the treacherous black barrel staring me down.

A diabolical sparkle filled her eyes as she squeezed the trigger again.

This time, the gun didn't go off.

The cartridge from the first round had gotten sideways in the ejection port, jamming the weapon.

I took the opportunity to sweep her legs from underneath her with a swift kick. She collapsed to the ground, and I summoned all of my strength and pounced on her. I wrestled the weapon away and pinned her to the ground. I dug into my pocket and slapped the cuffs around her wrists.

"You can't arrest me! You're an intruder in my home. You don't have a warrant!"

"That presents a bit of a situation, doesn't it? That grimoire connects you to the murder of your sister."

"Which is now inadmissible," she said with confidence.

"Go ahead and call the cops," I said. "I'll wait here until they show up. You'll invite them in, and they'll see the book in plain view, then it will be admissible."

She said nothing.

"You want me to call them for you?" I asked.

She kept quiet.

"I should tell you that your hair was found on the dagger that killed your sister. That, combined with the grimoire in your possession, will put you away for a long time if the police show up." I let that sink in. "What happened? Did you get jealous of your older sister? Mad because she inherited the bookstore. Mad because everything went her way."

"She didn't deserve it," Gwen said.

"And you did?"

"You're damn right."

There was a knock at the door.

It startled both of us.

A woman outside shouted, "Gwen. Are you all right?"

She'd heard the gunshot.

"What's it going to be?" I asked. "Are you going to jail for the rest of your life, or are you going to forget this little incident took place?"

"I'm not going to jail," Gwen hissed.

"Gwen!" the neighbor shouted again.

"Answer her," I demanded.

"I'll be right there!"

In a low growl, I said, "Go to the door and tell her your gun went off accidentally. Everything's okay."

Gwen hesitated.

"Do we have a deal?"

She grunted, "We have a deal."

I released the cuffs and kept the weapon aimed at her as she crawled off the floor. She stood up, hustled to the door, and pulled it open.

"I'm such an idiot," Gwen said to the neighbor. "I was handling the gun. It went off. It shot the wall. I'm so glad nobody got hurt."

She deserved an Academy Award.

"Gwen, you need to be more careful," the neighbor said, her voice shifting from concern to anger. "These walls are thin. You could have killed somebody. You could have killed me!"

"I know. I'm so sorry."

Apparently, the woman lived above her.

I grabbed the book, pulled on the mask, and snatched the spent cartridge. I climbed out the bedroom window while they continued to speak. I tried not to look conspicuous, walking through the grounds with an evil grimoire under my arm, Gwen's weapon in my pocket.

I left the apartment complex, ducked into an alley, peeled off the mask, and slipped out of the coveralls. I ditched them in the dumpster, hopped on my bicycle I'd locked up in the alley, and pedaled back to the *Avventura*.

My chest ached, and I was reminded of that with each bump and jolt in the road.

Buddy barked and growled when I boarded the boat. I don't know if he could sense the recent turmoil or if he didn't like the grimoire. I shouted, "Prim. Are you still here?"

"I'm in the kitchen."

"Galley. It's called a galley."

I hustled to meet her.

Her eyes rounded, and she gasped when I displayed the grimoire. "How did you get that?"

"Don't ask. Now, how do we get rid of it?"

49

I wasn't keen on destroying evidence. But something told me the world would be a better place without this monstrosity.

Prim told me it could only be destroyed in the fires of the Dracaena Cinnabari tree, otherwise known as Dragon's Blood. A fitting name, given the situation. A rare tree found in an archipelago in Yemen. A long way from Coconut Key.

The powdered sap was a popular item among the occult, and Gwen thought that might be enough.

I figured with enough lighter fluid, the damn thing would burn no matter what.

Gwen sprinkled the crimson powder between the pages of the evil manuscript. We had returned to her house to get it. I placed the grimoire in the barbecue grill in the backyard and doused the Codex with charcoal starter.

The sharp smell wafted.

I tossed in a match, and the book went up in flames. It popped and crackled, withering into blackened, charred ashes and glowing embers. Centuries of chaos were finally put to rest.

The book didn't cry out. Thunder didn't roll, wind didn't swirl. It didn't emit some type of mystical energy. It burned like an ordinary book.

I felt ridiculous for indulging in the process. But it would always haunt me if I let the book survive, and JD did not. Prim's warnings had been too grave and dire.

I poked it with a stick and stirred the ashes, dousing it with kerosene once again to make sure there were no traces of the grimoire left.

Prim seemed relieved.

We returned to the hospital. To my surprise, the entire gang was still there. They hadn't left JD's side. The band had commandeered chairs from other areas and camped out. Scarlett sat bedside, clasping JD's hand. The ventilator still wheezed, and the craggy peaks of his heartbeat blipped the monitor.

"How is he doing?" I asked.

Scarlett shook her head. "The same."

I introduced her to Prim. She recognized Scarlett but didn't make mention of it.

We stayed for a while, then I brought Prim back to the *Avventura*. I told her she could stay again, but I wanted to be at the hospital. I wasn't going to leave JD's side. The nurse was a good sport and helped me find another chair. It wasn't the most comfortable thing in the world, but I dozed off here and there, catching catnaps.

The nurse was in and out all night.

Morning sun crept through the blinds, casting shafts of amber rays across the room. I'd gotten about all the sleep that I could manage in the chair, so I went down to the cafeteria, grabbed a cup of coffee and some institutional eggs and soggy bacon. I chowed down, still trying to process everything that had happened, wondering if I had broken into someone's apartment and destroyed evidence for nothing. It seemed idiotic by the light of day. I hadn't been in my right mind.

The sheriff called. "How's he doing?"

"The same."

Daniels let out a disappointed sigh. "Brenda says you've got a theory about Cassandra Ravenwood's killer. She says you think the sister did it."

"Let's just say I'm 100% positive."

"What do you want to do about it?"

"I just need a strand of her hair."

"I'm sure you'll think of a creative way to get it."

"I'm sure."

I had a strand of her hair. But I wasn't going to lie about how I had acquired it. I needed to get it through legitimate means. Hopefully, it would be enough to tie her to the crime, even without the grimoire.

Daniels continued. "I guess Pablo's mother got tired of sitting in a jail cell."

"She give up her son?"

"Not exactly. But she did give me the name of his girlfriend. I knew you were preoccupied, so I sent Erickson and Faulkner to talk to her. The girlfriend came clean. She talked to Pablo. He's hiding out on Crystal Key. Get down to the station. We'll head out there with Erickson and Faulkner and pick that little bastard up."

50

The aluminum patrol boat carved through the swells, heading out toward Crystal Key. Mists of salt water sprayed, and the engines howled as the boat skimmed across the teal water.

The former owner of Crystal Key had grand plans for the island. It was supposed to be a luxury resort with all the amenities—quaint cabanas, recreational activities, and five-star dining. Paradise within paradise. But the project was never completed, and the island sat empty for years. Nature made short work of reclaiming its property.

Now the island was home to the occasional vagrant or kids looking for a place to party. It had also become a rendezvous point for illicit drug deals.

When we reached the island, Daniels circled around, surveying the coastline. We found a 25-foot center console anchored in the shallows at the south shore.

"I'll bet that's the boat reported stolen a few days ago from Pirates' Cove," Daniels said.

He called in the registration number on the vessel, and indeed, the owner had reported the vessel stolen.

We pulled alongside, and I hopped out of the patrol boat. I splashed into the surf and took a look at the craft. It had been hot-wired, which wasn't terribly hard to do on a boat like this.

Daniels anchored in the surf, and the rest of the team hopped out and advanced across the beach to the tree line.

The small island was thick with foliage. The original resort complex was overgrown and dilapidated. The pool was a nasty swamp of green algae-ridden sludge. A breeding pit for mosquitoes.

Beyond the main complex, a series of stilted cabanas.

With weapons drawn, we advanced through the underbrush to the main compound and surrounded what was once supposed to be the lobby. Only the dilapidated structure remained. The doors had long since been removed, and the windows broken out. It was supposed to house several dining options, a hip bar, a day spa, an athletic center, and even a beauty salon.

Now it was a roach-infested rat trap.

We approached the structure, and I held up at the main entrance. The sheriff and I flanked the doorway. I angled my rifle inside and clicked on the beam of my tactical flashlight, sweeping my barrel across the area.

It was dusty, musty, and full of cobwebs and debris. The entire structure, inside and out, had been tagged with graffiti—some of it creative, and some of it just unimaginative gang signs.

Daniels and I entered the main lobby and moved through the dank space while Erickson and Faulkner circled the structure outside.

The floor was littered with empty beer cans and bottles, hypodermic needles, and cigarette butts. There were a few stained mattresses where people had squatted. I couldn't imagine who would want to shelter in this place. I was surprised the entire structure hadn't burned down. All it would take was one cigarette butt. There were multiple holes in the walls where people had kicked or punched the rotting drywall. Some of the sheetrock was stained with mold, and I was convinced the air in here wasn't healthy to breathe.

We cleared the structure, then rejoined Erickson and Faulkner outside.

I figured Pablo might be hiding out in one of the cabanas. Some of them were in decent shape, while others were rotting and decaying. After multiple hurricanes, some were without roofs.

We followed the overgrown asphalt path that was lined with cracks and faded from the sun. It led to the cabanas where several structures dotted an overgrown meadow.

We followed the path, lined with trees and foliage, then stepped into the clearing.

As we did, gunshots erupted from the window of one of the cabanas. Muzzle flash flickered, and bullets snapped through the air.

We all scampered for cover behind trees at the edge of the meadow.

Pablo had no intention of surrendering without a fight.

51

I didn't particularly want to shoot the kid, but if you don't want to get shot, don't shoot at cops. Just a little pro tip.

We lit up the cabana with a volley of gunfire. Bullets impacted against the siding, splattering fragments of wood.

Pablo ducked for cover.

The gunfire settled for a moment, and the meadow was silent.

Clouds of smoke drifted through the air.

I didn't know if Pablo was hit or out of ammo. It was hard to say what he had in that cabana and how long he could hold out.

A few minutes later, the door flung open, and he plunged down the creaky wooden steps. One of the boards cracked under his foot, and he almost tumbled down the last few steps.

He sprinted toward the nearest tree line, heading for the west beach. He darted into the underbrush, and I sprinted through the trees to cut him off.

Leaves rustled, and twigs snapped under my feet as I barreled through the thick jungle. I raced toward the shore and held up at the edge of the beach. I figured Pablo would circle back around, trying to make it to the boat. I was between him and his destination, crouching in the underbrush.

Sapphire waves crashed against the shore. Gulls hung on the draft.

Pablo approached my position but caught sight of me. He aimed his pistol and fired two more rounds. The barrel flickered, and bullets snapped through the air.

I hugged a tree trunk for cover, and Pablo spun around, running down the beach in the opposite direction.

I darted onto the white sand, chasing after him, kicking up sand as I ran. My chest heaved for breath, and my legs drove me forward. Each inhale stung, a painful reminder of my misguided deed.

Pablo angled his pistol back at me and snapped off another round. The bullet cracked through the air and zipped past my ear.

I really didn't want to get shot twice within a 24-hour time frame. I'd gotten lucky once.

Then I got lucky again.

Pablo was out of ammunition.

Frustration tensed his face, and he tossed the pistol away and kept running down the beach.

I kept after him, running as fast as I could.

The little bastard was quick.

But I was gaining on him.

Erickson and Faulkner were several paces behind.

Daniels hadn't even bothered. He left that crap to the young guys.

Pablo kept running, but he had nowhere to go.

He cut back into the underbrush.

The foliage was too thick to cut across from where I was.

I kept running down the beach, then into the trees where he had entered. Pablo weaved through the trunks, hopping fallen logs and dodging low branches. He made a hell of a ruckus, spooking birds and other wildlife.

I kept gaining on him.

He hit a cross trail and veered left, heading toward the north shore.

I followed.

Pablo kept looking over his shoulder with wide eyes as I stuck with him.

He hit the north beach and took a right.

I kept sprinting after him.

The little punk wasn't used to this kind of thing. A quick dash here and there, but he wasn't an endurance runner. He didn't have the lungs for it.

I caught up with him on the beach and tackled him to the ground. He pulled a knife and slashed at me.

I caught his forearm before the blade could carve into me.

I twisted his arm in a position it didn't want to be in, and his grasp on the knife went slack. It fell into the sand, and I subdued the punk and slapped the cuffs around his wrists.

"You're under arrest for the murder of Teresa Gomez," I said. "You have the right to remain silent..."

"Fuck you!" he grumbled, his face in the sand.

I patted him down, checking for additional weapons.

He was clean.

I yanked him to his feet and marched him back to the clearing. I ran into Erickson and Faulkner along the way, and we eventually rejoined the sheriff.

We searched the cabana and found a bag of marijuana, junk food, sodas, and beer. He had a little stockpile, but it wouldn't have lasted long.

We marched him back to the patrol boat and transferred him aboard.

I hopped into the center console, fired up the engine, and followed the sheriff back to Coconut Key.

One happy owner would get his boat back.

52

"**G**ood evening," Vivian said. "Thanks for coming." She stepped aside and motioned us into the foyer.

I entered and introduced the girls. "Prim is a highly regarded psychic medium, and Teagan assisted the department in the capture of the Island Skinner."

"Impressive," Vivian said. "It's a pleasure to meet you both."

She shook hands with the girls.

"I'm just going to go on record and say that this is nonsense," Devon barked. "But for Vivian's sake, I've agreed to it."

Vivian gave him a look, then introduced the girls to Landon. "I felt it was best for the whole family to be here for this."

"It's important to have a strong connection," Prim said. "The more loved ones, the better." She added, "It's also important that everyone believe. If you don't believe, please try to abstain from thinking negative thoughts. The spirits can feel that, and it could make them more hesitant to communicate."

Devon stifled an eye-roll.

Landon looked nervous and unsettled.

Prim picked up on it. "Don't worry. There's nothing to be afraid of. I don't expect us to encounter any malevolent spirits tonight."

I had coached the girls, and they knew what to say. We weren't conducting a real seánce. We were just trying to draw out a killer.

"Where do you want to do this?" Vivian asked.

"The kitchen table," Prim said. "It's as good a place as any. Symbolic of a family gathering. What more appropriate of a place than to request the presence of Lily?" She flashed a reassuring smile.

Vivian's eyes brimmed as she nodded. "Right this way."

She escorted us through the living room and into the kitchen. We all took a seat around the table, and Prim pulled a candle from her bag and placed it in the center of the table. She lit the candle and a stick of incense in a wooden tray. Wisps of spicy smoke swirled, and the air filled with the fragrant aroma, mixed with the scent of wax and vanilla from the candle.

"Would you mind turning out the light?" Prim said to Landon.

He did.

"And the patio and pool lights, please."

Landon did as she asked, then returned to the table.

With everyone seated, Prim asked, "Shall we begin?"

"Yes, please," Vivian replied with enthusiasm.

"Please clasp hands, and remember, no negative energy," Prim said as she began to lead the faux séance. The amber glow of the candlelight flickered on her face, casting long shadows. "I'd like to begin this session by declaring our intentions. We are here to communicate with the spirits of the departed, including Lily and others who may linger in this domain."

Devon made a face.

Prim continued. She chanted something in an ancient, forgotten tongue. Perhaps she made it up. Either way, it made for a good show. She closed her eyes, took a deep breath, then exhaled. "Lily, I'm here with your family. They desperately want to speak with you. They have unresolved questions that only you can answer. We beg you to communicate with us. If you're here, flicker the candle flame."

All eyes fell upon the steady flame, its reflection glimmering in the eyes of those around the table.

It remained steady for a moment, then flickered for an instant.

It drew an audible gasp from Vivian.

I watched with amusement.

Anything could have caused the flame to flicker—the air conditioning kicking on, a draft in the room, the breath of one of the participants at the table. Perhaps Prim and Teagan were working in conjunction. All eyes were focused on Prim. Teagan could have blown the candle from the side of her mouth.

"Thank you," Prim said. "Is there anyone else here with you?"

The candle flame flickered again.

"Who else is here with you?"

The candle flame flickered again and went out.

Vivian shrieked.

"It's okay," Prim said in a soothing voice. She sparked her lighter, and the flame danced. She re-lit the candle.

Teagan gasped. "Alaric and Jasper."

She looked terrified, really selling it.

This was starting to get good.

Vivian leaned in with curious eyes. "Jasper's here?"

Teagan nodded, looking mortified, her eyes round. "He was murdered in this house, along with Alaric."

Devon shook his head dismissively. "Enough of this nonsense. Somebody turn on the light."

"Who killed them?" Vivian asked.

Teagan looked astonished as the revelation washed over her. She pointed her finger at Landon.

I lifted a surprised brow. That's not how we rehearsed this.

53

"You poisoned Jasper," Teagan continued. Then she looked at Devon. "You came home, saw that Jasper was dead, and helped Landon dispose of the body." She glanced back to Landon. "You killed Alaric because you thought he learned the truth."

Panic filled the kid's eyes. He pushed his chair away from the table and sprinted through the kitchen. He grabbed a butcher knife from a wooden holder containing a set. The blade chimed as he drew it and glimmered with the reflection of the candlelight.

I launched from the table and took a few steps toward him.

Landon angled around the butcher block, keeping it between us.

Devon flicked on the light.

Vivian shouted, "Landon, put that knife down!"

"I'm not going to jail." His frantic eyes darted about.

Devon's eyes grew dark. He looked at his son. "Landon, just take it easy," he said in a calm voice. "Nobody's going to jail."

Devon pulled a pistol from the small of his back and aimed at me.

The girls gasped.

Vivian shouted, "Devon, what are you doing!?"

"Shut up, Vivian!"

The situation had gone from bad to worse.

Devon moved around the table, keeping the weapon aimed at me as he stepped closer. "Put your hands in the air, deputy. Keep them where I can see them."

I complied.

"Landon, put the knife down and take the deputy's weapon. Do it. Now!"

The knife clattered as he set it on the butcher block near Vivian's expensive purse. Landon moved around the marble slab and took my pistol that was holstered in my waistband. He didn't notice the small subcompact in my cargo pocket.

Now I had two weapons aimed at me, one considerably more twitchy than the other. Landon's eyes flicked between me and his father, the gun barrel shaking.

"What are you two doing!?" Vivian screeched.

"Just stay put and keep your mouth shut, Vivian. Nobody move or the deputy dies."

"You came home and saw that your son had killed Jasper," I said. "You didn't want to see him go to jail, so you helped him. The witness that saw Jasper leave on his boat didn't see Jasper. He saw your son. They look alike. Same height, hair coloring, same build."

"You're good, deputy. Too good."

"Apparently not good enough," I muttered.

"Everybody makes a mistake sometimes."

"Just out of curiosity, how do you see this whole scenario panning out? What are you going to do? Kill the three of us? Dump our bodies?"

"The thought had crossed my mind," Devon said, keeping his weapon steady, the barrel staring me down.

He was smart enough to keep his distance—out of striking reach.

"Are you okay with this, Vivian?" I asked.

"I most certainly am not!"

"Sounds like you've got a little problem, Devon," I said. "You think your wife will stay quiet? It's hard to keep secrets between two people, much less three."

"Vivian will keep her mouth shut," Devon assured. "She doesn't want her son to spend his life behind bars. Jasper was no good for my daughter. Landon did us all a favor. Jasper was just going to discard her and break her heart anyway. Did you know he had multiple other girlfriends on the island?"

"People know where we are," I said. "They'll come looking."

"You never showed up." He grinned.

"What are you going to do? Kill us all right here?"

Devon smiled. "No. I don't want to clean up the mess, and gunshots would draw too much attention, don't you think?"

I said nothing.

"It's such a nice evening. A great night for a boat ride." Devon looked at his son. "Landon, escort the ladies to the boat."

The kid moved around the butcher block and waved the gun at the girls. "Get up!"

They cautiously pushed away from the table and stood up. He grabbed Teagan's arm, pulled her close, and shoved the pistol into her rib cage. With the two close together, it might be hard for a neighbor to notice he had a gun on her.

"I don't need to tell you that if you try anything, my son will shoot one of your friends."

"You're going to kill us anyway," I said. "What's the difference?"

Devon glared at me. "If you want to do this a different way, perhaps another method of killing would be more acceptable to you?"

"You kill us here, you still have to get the bodies out of here and hope someone doesn't notice."

"You sure do talk a tough game, but I don't think you want to see those girls hurt, even if you know what eventually waits for you." He addressed his son. "Take them to the boat. Now!"

Landon escorted the girls out of the house and onto the patio.

"Now, deputy, are you going to go quietly?" Devon asked.

I said nothing.

Vivian hissed at Devon. "This is insane. What are you doing!?"

"Vivian, you're going to stay here and keep your mouth shut. When I come back, we will never speak of this again."

"When you come back, you and I will never speak again."

"You think it's wise to threaten a man who's capable of murdering two women and a deputy? At this point, what's the harm in adding a fourth to the mix?"

Vivian gasped in a mix of rage and horror. Hatred filled her.

"On second thought, you're coming with us," Devon said.

"No, I am not."

"Vivian, now is not the time to argue," he said in a low growl.

I still had my hands in the air while the two argued.

Vivian was silent a moment, then relented. "I just need to get my purse."

"You don't need your purse. This will be a quick trip."

It rested on the butcher block not far from the kitchen knife.

54

Vivian defied him and moved to her purse. She grabbed it from the butcher block as Devon let out an exasperated sigh. She swung the purse with all her might, clocking him in the face. The heavy bag knocked him to the ground, and I took my opportunity to strike.

I pounced on him, grabbed the gun, and wrestled it away from him before he could recover. I sprang to my feet, stepped away from him, and took aim.

By this time, Landon and the girls had passed the pool and the spires of evergreens and were halfway to the dock. The yard sloped down toward the canal, and from Landon's vantage point, it would be hard to see the commotion in the house.

I commanded Devon to turn around and put his hands behind his head.

Devon scowled at me but complied.

I pulled my cuffs from my pocket and tossed them to Vivian. "Cuff him."

"With pleasure."

She slapped the cuffs around his wrists and ratcheted them extra tight.

Devon winced.

I told her to dial 911, then went after Landon and the girls.

I sprinted outside, chasing after the punk.

Landon had reached the wake boat, and Prim had boarded. He looked back over his shoulder and saw me. A mix of anger and concern tensed his face. He put the gun to Teagan's head and stood behind her. "Stay back, or she dies!"

I froze in my tracks.

The next-door neighbor was on the dock and saw the whole thing. He stared in disbelief with wide eyes.

"Put the gun down now before anybody else gets hurt," I said.

He shuffled Teagan onto the boat and climbed aboard. He demanded she cast off the lines, and he told Prim to take the helm and start the engine. The twin inboards rumbled to life, and water at the stern burbled and bubbled.

I advanced toward the boat.

Landon kept his pistol aimed at Teagan and stayed close. He forced Prim to pull away from the dock.

She complied and throttled up.

I sprinted down to the dock as the boat raced away. The engines growled as it hauled ass through the *no wake zone*. Tumultuous waves splashed against hulls, rocking boats, pressing them to their limits against fenders.

I flashed my badge to the neighbor. "I need your boat."

We'd met briefly before when we canvassed the area.

He shook his head. "Nobody drives my boat but me."

He climbed aboard and took the helm.

I cast off the lines and hopped in with him as he fired up the five mercury outboards.

We pulled away from the dock, and the neighbor throttled up. We raced through the canal, chasing after the little wake boat.

They cleared the breakwater and hit the ocean.

We weren't far behind, and it didn't take long to catch up. The boat plowed through the inky swells, and Landon grew agitated that we were right on his tail. It was a little choppy, and the boats bounced and skipped across the water.

Landon displayed Teagan at the stern with the gun to her head—a warning for me to stay away.

Prim cut the throttle, and the two tumbled forward.

Teagan grabbed a wakeboard from the deck. She came up with it and pummeled Landon as he staggered to his feet. The smack echoed across the water.

Landon tumbled back against the dash.

The girls pounced on him, and not in the way you'd like those two to pounce. They struggled for the gun, and my heart leapt into my throat.

We pulled alongside the boat, and I jumped aboard.

Landon was a big kid. Lean and muscular. He bucked the two petite girls off with relative ease and came up with the gun.

He climbed to his feet and drew down on Teagan.

Prim throttled up, and the boat lurched forward.

Landon tumbled toward the stern. He hit the deck, and his pistol clattered aft.

I had my backup drawn. "Don't move!"

Landon hesitated, then his jaw tightened. He chose *death-by-cop* and charged me.

I really didn't want to shoot the kid.

I hunkered down and readied my stance. I absorbed the charge, sidestepped, pivoted, and used his momentum to ram him into the seat at the stern.

Landon pushed off the cushions and spun around.

I pistol-whipped him, shattering his nose, spewing blood. He fell back onto the seat.

While he was dazed, I holstered my pistol, grabbed his shirt, and threw him to the deck. I pounced and put a knee into his back and ratcheted the cuffs around his wrists. "You're under arrest for the murders of Alaric Vesper and Jasper Armstrong."

I read him his rights, and Prim navigated us back to the mansion.

The neighbor followed.

By the time we arrived, first responders had swarmed the area. Red and blue lights flickered out front, and deputies waited on the dock.

Paris and her news crew were on the scene. The cameraman grabbed footage of me escorting Landon ashore. I handed him over to the deputies, and they dragged him to a squad car. I helped the frazzled ladies disembark.

I told the neighbor he'd get a commendation.

He smiled with pride, puffing up his chest.

"Happy to help," he said.

We shook hands, and the camera closed in.

Paris interviewed me, the neighbor, and the girls. I think they enjoyed being in the spotlight for a moment. But that didn't keep Teagan from growling at me afterward. "Why do you always get me into these kinds of situations?"

"I don't get you into these situations. They just happen."

Prim smiled. "I thought it was kind of exciting."

"You didn't have a gun to your head," Teagan said. Her teal eyes found me again. "You owe me, mister. Big time!"

"I'm good for it," I assured with a smile.

I walked the girls across the back lawn toward the pool. "You both did a superb job. That was better than we rehearsed.

But what made you change it up and point the finger at Landon?"

Teagan gave me a flat look. "Jasper and Alaric both told me he was the one responsible."

I gave her a doubtful look.

"I'm serious."

"I thought you weren't a medium," I said, skeptical.

"So did I. I guess I have another gift to worry about."

I dismissed the notion. "You're just messing with me, and it's not gonna work."

"How else could I have known?"

I didn't have an answer.

Prim smiled. "Always a skeptic."

I shrugged. "What can I say?"

"Would I lie to you?" Teagan asked.

"No."

"I'm not lying. Believe whatever you want to believe. I'm not changing my story."

The girls piled into the 1970 Plum Crazy Purple Barracuda, affectionately dubbed the *Devastator*. I drove Teagan to her apartment and dropped her off, then drove Prim back to her house. I'd held to my word and fixed the back door for her. I'd enjoyed her company on the boat, but I wasn't quite ready for a permanent house guest. She wasn't either.

I parked at the curb and escorted her to the front porch.

"This was a good night," Prim said with an optimistic glimmer in her eyes. "Want to come in?"

"I'd love to, but I need to fill out reports and stop by the hospital to check on JD."

"Some other time, then."

"Absolutely."

She lifted on her tiptoes and gave me a kiss. "I had fun."

"Fun?"

"I'm learning to embrace chaos."

I laughed.

"I think I've lived in fear for too long. Perhaps more exploration of the unknown is warranted."

"Are you going to start channeling spirits more often?" I teased.

She paused. "To tell you the truth. I didn't sense any spirits tonight. That was all Teagan."

"Hmm," I mumbled curiously.

Prim fumbled for the key and unlocked the door. "Goodnight, deputy."

She slipped inside, and I jogged to the car and headed to the station to fill out after-action reports. Afterward, I went to the hospital to check on JD.

He'd definitely taken a turn.

55

Jack was wide awake, like nothing had ever happened. The ventilator had been removed, and he was looking chipper, holding court.

I breathed a huge sigh of relief. "Good to see you back among the land of the living."

"Good to be here."

Scarlett was still by his side, as well as the band. They hadn't left.

"What the hell was wrong with you?" I asked.

Jack shrugged. "Parker came by earlier. He thinks it was some kind of bacterial infection. They pumped me full of antibiotics. He said they're still waiting on a culture. All I know is I'm ready to get the hell out of here."

"When does that happen?"

"I want it to happen right now, but Parker wants to keep me overnight, just in case."

"I think that's probably a good idea."

"Where are we at with everything?"

I caught him up to speed, but I left out the part about the grimoire. I didn't think anybody else would believe it. I'm not sure I believed it myself.

Scarlett had been there all day, and she was ready to go. She said her goodbyes to Jack and told him she'd be back in the morning.

The guys bid him farewell and left when we did.

I drove Scarlett back to Diver Down. She said she wanted to stay aboard the boat tonight. We stopped at Diver Down to grab something to eat. Alejandro was behind the bar.

A repeat of Paris Delaney's broadcast from the Trask mansion flashed on the screen.

Scarlett was still incognito with sunglasses and a ball cap, but a few people recognized her and approached for an autograph. She was gracious about it, but she was worn out.

We took our food to go and chowed down on the sky deck of the *Avventura*. She told me all about her upcoming projects and caught me up to speed on current events in Los Angeles.

Prim buzzed my phone.

"Are you missing the Avventura already?" I teased.

"Remember what I said about embracing chaos? Yeah, well, I'm gonna take that back."

"What's the matter?"

"Well, there's a cloaked ghoul in my house with a gun to my head who says if you don't bring the grimoire, she's going to kill me." Then she added, "Oh, and by the way, you'll have to fix the back door glass again."

My jaw tensed. I had no doubt that the woman in the ghoulish costume was Gwen. She'd broken into the back door and waited for Prim to arrive.

"Let me speak with the ghoul," I said.

She handed over the phone, and Gwen's voice filtered through. She didn't even bother trying to disguise it. "You have half an hour, or Prim dies. You tell any of your cop buddies about this, she dies. Come alone. Bring the grimoire."

She ended the call.

I had bad news for her. She was going to be massively disappointed.

56

Since the grimoire was no longer in existence, I had nothing to trade. I needed a stand-in. Something that resembled the dark book.

I called Sybil.

"My lawyer says not to talk to you," she replied.

"You got a lawyer?"

"I thought a consultation was the prudent thing to do since you did come into my store asking pointed questions. I've seen those shows on TV where an innocent person gets railroaded."

"Don't worry. I know you didn't kill Cassandra."

She paused. "Is this some kind of weird ploy to get me to confess?"

"No. I need a favor."

"That sounds interesting," she said in a sultry tone.

"I need to borrow or buy a grimoire."

"Dabbling in the occult?"

"I've dabbled enough. Let's just say I need a look-alike for the real thing. As I recall, you told me about some knockoffs in your store."

"I don't know if they will pass muster, but at a quick glance, maybe."

"That's all it's going to be is a quick glance."

"When someone opens the book, they'll know right away it's not the real thing," Sybil warned. "Did you ever find it, by the way?"

"I can neither confirm nor deny."

"That sounds intriguing. I'd like to hear more."

"Some other time, perhaps."

"Perhaps."

"I've got a couple of the grimoires in the store. Want to come in tomorrow? No charge."

"This is an emergency situation. I need one tonight. As in now."

"I'm kind of in the middle of something, but this sounds like an emergency."

"It is." I gave her the details.

"In that case, I'll meet you at the bookstore in 15 minutes."

I ended the call and got my ass to *Arcana & Alchemy* as soon as possible. I arrived before she did and waited on the sidewalk in front of the store.

Sybil showed up a few moments later, the keys jingling in her hand. She unlocked the door and invited me in.

I followed Sybil as she moved through the shop to one of the bookshelves and grabbed the knockoff. She handed it to me. "Do you think this will pass?"

My face tightened with indecision. "Maybe. It's a little lighter, not quite the same dimensions, and it lacks centuries of wear."

"That's all I've got."

I thumbed through the pages. The book was printed on a cream-colored approximation of parchment. It wasn't a grimoire of actual spells from the original book. It was a text *about* the grimoire and speculations on what was inside. Of course, there were a few sigils and incantations that were thought to be in the Obsidian Codex, but the whole thing was just the imagination of the author. A money grab, trying to cash in on the allure of the mystical book.

"What do I owe you for this?"

Her eyes narrowed as she contemplated it. Sybil lifted a naughty eyebrow. "How about you give me an IOU? I'll collect on a later date when I'm in need."

It was a little open-ended for my taste, but beggars can't be choosers.

There was one glaring difference between this knockoff and the real thing. It was missing a bullet hole in the cover.

I took the book into the back alley behind the store, dropped it on the concrete, pulled out my pistol, and took aim.

The gunshot echoed, and muzzle flash illuminated my face. Wisps of smoke drifted from the barrel.

Dogs barked in the distance, disturbed by the noise.

I picked up the book. The slug had gone three-quarters of the way through. Now it was about as authentic as it was going to get.

"You have something against that book?" Sybil asked, witnessing the whole thing.

"It needs to look authentic."

Sybil lifted a curious brow. "The real Codex has a bullet in it?"

"Had," I said.

She pondered my vague statement.

I thanked her again, hopped into the Devastator, and drove to Prim's house. I parked at the curb and dialed her phone as I arrived.

Gwen answered.

"I'm here with the book," I said. "Let Prim go, and I'll leave the book at the curb. Send her out through the front door."

"No," Gwen replied. "You don't get the girl until I've had a chance to examine the book. Come in through the back door. It's unlocked. I'm in the living room with Prim. Do not bring a weapon. If anyone else is with you or any cops show up, she dies. Are we clear?"

"If she dies, you'll never get the book."

"Well, it seems like we both have something to lose." She ended the call.

I killed the engine and hopped out of the Devastator. No way I was going in there without a weapon. It was holstered in my waistband for an appendix carry, and my untucked T-shirt was enough to conceal the weapon.

I walked up the dark driveway. The lights in the house were off except for the living room, which was lit by candlelight. The flames flickered, dancing, painting fluid shadows on the walls.

The back door creaked as I pushed it open. The pane that I had replaced earlier had been shattered, and my shoes crunched against the shards of glass that glimmered on the tile. "It's me. I'm coming in."

I made my way into the living room.

Prim stood with terrified eyes as Gwen held a pistol to her head. She was still dressed in the ghoulish robe and mask and used Prim as a shield.

"This is twice in one night, deputy," Prim said.

"Sorry about that."

"Show me the grimoire," Gwen demanded.

I held up the book, displaying the cover with the bullet hole.

In the dim candlelight, looking through a cheap mask with slits for eyeholes, I figured Gwen's vision wasn't a hundred percent.

"Toss the book to me, and I'll let her go," the ghoul said.

I threw the book onto the floor, halfway between us.

Gwen didn't like that too much.

"Now let her go."

Gwen hesitated a moment, then pushed Prim toward me. Her wrists were bound behind her back with rope. She stumbled away, and I commanded, "Exit the house by the front door. Now!"

She did, struggling to open the front door.

Gwen kept her weapon aimed at me as she inched toward the book. "Don't move!"

She squatted down and reached a hand for the book.

G wen instantly realized the grimoire was a fake.

She growled and squeezed the trigger at close range.

Flames flickered from the barrel.

Bullets snapped across the living room.

I drew my weapon and returned fire, putting two slugs into her chest.

Gwen tumbled back and squeezed off another round, the bullet rocketing into the ceiling, spraying bits of gypsum. The debris fluttered to the ground as she writhed and moaned in agony, gurgling for breath.

I rushed to her, kicked the pistol away, and holstered my weapon. She gasped her last breath as I knelt beside her.

I peeled off her mask, and her cold eyes stared at the ceiling. The color drained from her skin and lips, and she looked older now and certainly not at peace. Torment tensed her lifeless face. And I figured she was well on her way to some-where she'd rather not be.

I called the sheriff and updated him on the situation. It wasn't long before deputies and responders swarmed the property. Brenda and her crew arrived. Prim and I gave full statements. I was put on administrative leave pending an investigation.

Daniels gave me an earful about handling the situation without backup, and he was probably right.

Prim was a little shaken. Understandably so. In light of recent events, she decided to stay on the *Avventura* for another night. That was fine by me. We had some demons to work out.

Jack got sprung in the morning. Parker told him to take it easy, rest, and avoid alcohol for a while.

JD took none of it to heart.

Scarlett stayed in town for Halloween and hung out back-stage with us for the big show. Oyster Avenue was packed, and revelers filled the street, sporting all sorts of costumes. There were naughty nurses, ghoulish demons, little devils in short skirts, sexy vampires, monsters, aliens, and more.

When it was time, I hit the stage, took the mic, and shouted, "Please welcome to the stage... the mighty... Wild Fury!"

The crowd erupted with cheers and whistles, hoots and hollers.

Dizzy struck a power cord as the band rushed on stage, dressed as spooky ghosts with twisted pale faces. Styxx took his place behind the drum kit, and Crash thumped on bass.

JD made a grand entrance, and the crowd went wild. He lifted his mask and screamed into the microphone, "Happy Halloween! Are you ready to rock 'n' roll?"

The question was met with a resounding roar of enthusiasm.

I don't know why JD had gotten so sick or how he had made his miraculous recovery. Jack never mentioned anything about it afterward. I'm sure Dr. Parker followed up with him, but I never heard the results of the culture.

The band put on a helluva show, and JD sang his heart out. You'd never know he was in the hospital with respiratory failure just the day before. It was nothing short of amazing.

In the morning, we hit Waffle Wizard, and I finally got to indulge in the blueberry waffles I'd been craving.

Toward the end of the meal, Jack's phone buzzed. A sobbing girl's voice filtered through the speaker when he answered. There was no mistaking her emotional pain. "Jack, I need your help!"

"What's going on?"

Ready for more?

The adventure continues with Wild West!

Join my newsletter and find out what happens next!

AUTHOR'S NOTE

Thanks for taking this incredible journey with me. I'm having such a blast writing about Tyson and JD, and I've got plenty more adventures to come. I hope you'll stick around for the wild ride.

Thanks for all the great reviews and kind words!

If you liked this book, let me know with a review on Amazon.

Thanks for reading!

—Tripp

TYSON WILD

Wild Ocean

Wild Justice

Wild Rivera

Wild Tide

Wild Rain

Wild Captive

Wild Killer

Wild Honor

Wild Gold

Wild Case

Wild Crown

Wild Break

Wild Fury

Wild Surge

Wild Impact

Wild L.A.

Wild High

Wild Abyss

Wild Life

Wild Spirit

Wild Thunder

Wild Season

Wild Rage

Wild Heart

Wild Spring

Wild Outlaw

Wild Revenge

Wild Secret

Wild Envy

Wild Surf

Wild Venom

Wild Island

Wild Demon

Wild Blue

Wild Lights

Wild Target

Wild Jewel

Wild Greed

Wild Sky

Wild Storm

Wild Bay

Wild Chaos

Wild Cruise

Wild Catch

Wild Encounter

Wild Blood

Wild Vice

Wild Winter

Wild Malice

Wild Fire

Wild Deceit

Wild Massacre

Wild Illusion

Wild Mermaid

Wild Star

Wild Skin

Wild Prodigy

Wild Sport

Wild Hex

Wild West

Wild...

CONNECT WITH ME

I'm just a geek who loves to write. Follow me on Facebook.

www.trippellis.com

f X ⓞ

Made in the USA
Middletown, DE
01 November 2023

41762312R00187